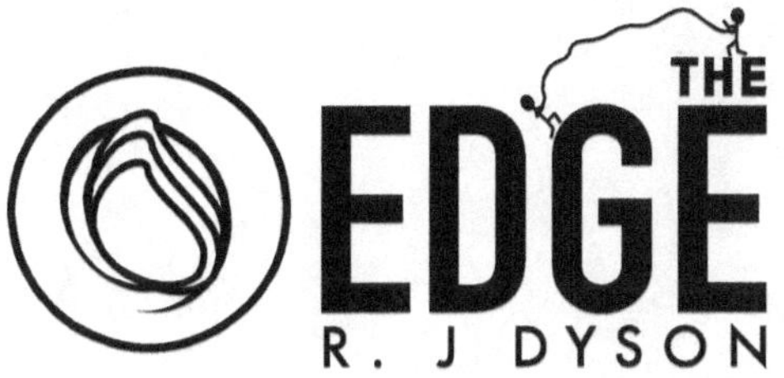

THE EDGE

R. J DYSON

absolutelyunprofessional.com
Wadsworth, OH

First Printing: 2022
ISBN 978-0-9997832-6-9
Absolutely Unprofessional
Wadsworth, OH 44281
absounpro.com
rjdysonsblog.com
absolutelyunprofessional.com

to my kids, and all those following
the glow on the edge

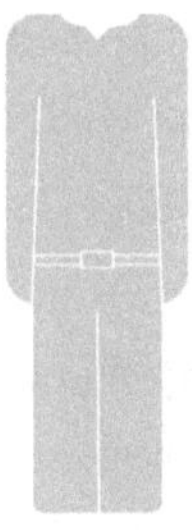

1 It Begins

"Reach for it!" cried Joanna.

"My shoulder's...gonna pop...out of joint...if I stretch...any...further." Heschel's uniform began pulling apart along the shoulder seam. Sweat seemed to travel directly into his eyes.

"We won't get another chance!" she said. "It's now or never."

"Aaaaggghhhh!" Heschel grabbed hold of the half-buried object, grit his teeth, and fell back into the side of the hill with a rush. Clinging to the rope with one hand while holding the object firmly with the other, he yelled, "Got it!"

Joanna cinched the line, took a deep breath, and pulled tight as her friend navigated the steep hillside in the dark.

"I've never been that close to the waterfall," said Heschel, one hand squeezing the rope and the other pressed by his side with the jagged object wedged beneath his armpit.

"I've never been to the edge," she said. "How far do you think the drop is?"

"I don't know, but I can't feel my fingers," he said, trying to make a fist. "What if I never type again? What if I can't press on the device in session? What happens when I'm called on to…"

"Are you hyperventilating? You've done more difficult exercises in training," said Joanna. "Are you feeling okay? Tell me, can you feel this?" she said, pinching the soft meaty flesh on the back of his arm.

"Ouch!" Heschel jumped back with a whimper, nearly dropping the item. He wasn't a wimp. After all, the whole adventure was his idea. It's just that he had never done anything rebellious before and couldn't tell if he was wildly excited or terrified.

After a few deep breaths and a snort that made them both laugh a little too hard, he asked, "So, what do you think it is?"

"A relic of the past. I've never seen these symbols before," she said. "Do you think this was done by hand? Could it be that ancient? Definitely before paper and tablets."

"It's strange, isn't it?" he said, tossing his sore arm around to get the blood flowing into each tingling digit. "We're holding a piece of history. A defunct and forgotten language. If we're not careful, we might even be in possession of an illegal idea."

"Look, we don't know what it is," said Joanna, tucking the object into a secret panel within her waist pack. "And we have no idea what it says. Illegal or not, we'd better get back before they notice we're missing. Do you think monitors patrol this far out?"

Heschel looked around the woods. The moonglow was exceptionally bright, making their venture more dangerous. Upriver, he saw a flash along the shore, like the reflection of moonlight off of a monitor's belt buckle. *Why does everything in the forest appear more sinister at night?* After a moment of staring, he decided it was nothing more than water splashing from the rocks.

"I doubt it," he said with a deep breath. "In fact, what are the odds we'd find something game-changing on our first exploration? After all, everything was destroyed, right? We've heard all the history The Chamber decided was worth knowing. Besides, why would they hide the past from us? Who would benefit?"

"I heard something about it once, I think," she said cautiously. "A few years ago, one of the hall monitors began to share a memory about an old family tradition."

"They actually said *family tradition?*" asked Heschel, looking into the treeline.

"They must have panicked when they saw me standing nearby because they demanded I drop and do fifty push-ups on the spot."

"Maybe you misunderstood them. *Handy munitions? Fancy rendition?* Have you heard them slip again?"

"I haven't seen that one since." Joanna looked back over both shoulders. She was beginning to feel uncomfortable outside the dorm at night. What if they were being tracked?

Heschel crouched low, pulling Joanna down onto the soft moss. "You didn't mention a disappeared monitor! That changes things. That changes everything!"

"Deep breaths, Heschel. Deep breaths. They were reassigned," she said, placing her hand on his shoulder without knowing why. After all, there were unspoken rules against that sort of camaraderie. Touching another human outside of training was unacceptable.

His chest heaved in and out. He sat up a little taller. "How do you know?"

"0561."

"Wait, what time is it? It's almost roll call!"

Joanna grabbed his sleeve mid-leap, pulling him back down to earth. "Their serial number. Not the time. I heard the replacement say that #0561 had been reassigned to the edge.”

“You can let go of my jacket now,” he said, dusting off while scurrying to his knees. “0561. Family tradition. The edge.” His pupils dilated in the moonlight. “Wait a second. We’re on the edge right now. What if they’re watching? They’re always watching.”

“No one’s watching. They have no reason to believe we’d be anywhere but our flat,” said Joanna, running her hands through the soft patch of moss between the forest line and the waterfall. Once again, she looked over both shoulders into the dark forest. “Have you heard anything like that before?”

“Family tradition? No. Well, tradition, yes, it’s all we do around here. Follow orders. Do what the students before us did. Don’t change a thing. Don’t be curious. Don’t ask.”

Joanna began to laugh. “Wow, I’ve never seen a face contort like that. What do you call it?”

“I call it my face. It’s full of muscles. It takes a lot of muscles to communicate.” Heschel’s voice rose and cracked, the sort of crack a voice does at his age. “Yours has been pretty fluid as well, ya know.”

“Expression. That’s what it is. Your face is all contorted and big and mushy. I’ve never seen you act so expressive before.” Immediately Joanna began feeling her cheeks and forehead for lumps and wrinkles.

“Yeah, well anyhow, I don’t know what the family part

is. How do families have traditions of their own?" He sat back down on the moss and began running his hands through it like hair. "I mean, all of our families sent us here. That's what parental units do. It's what we've always done. I don't know my biological faction, and I don't think about them. Do you?"

A quiet but steady beeping sound from a distance shook them both from their pondering. It was Joanna's alarm. She had set it just in case they lost track of time.

"Four hours 'til sunrise," she said. "Time to go. If we're not fully rested, they'll suspect something."

"I'll grab our devices beneath the leaf pile," Heschel said. "Let's hope they weren't tracking any of that."

 2 Rude Awakening

"**W**ake up!" Heschel was dressed and ready for roll call, which just so happened to be in five minutes. "Joanna!"

He had been executing his morning routine with all the others just like him at the other end of the floor when he lost track of time in the shower. Showers were short, only three minutes apiece. After seven minutes, he was startled from his daydream when the monitor threw open the door and turned off the water.

"What on the edge is going on in here?" The growl was rough but curious. "Are you ill, student?"

"What? What's happened on the edge? Who shut off the water?" His voice squeaked in confusion. The soap suds in his hair immediately ran into his eyes as he slipped back against the stall, falling to the floor.

"We're behind schedule," said the monitor staring down at him. "From here on out, two-minute showers for everyone. Step it up."

Heschel stumbled to his feet, grabbed his towel from the hook, and made his way to the sink to quickly rinse the soap from his hair and eyes. Five jumping jacks, five push-ups, and five sit-ups, no more and no less. Just enough to get the blood flowing. For the first time, he felt something heavy in the air around him. *Is this what anger feels like? Or maybe embarrassment? I've never been embarrassed before,* he thought.

"Hey, wake up already. We're going to get caught!"

"What time is it?" she said, pulling the stock issue gray blanket over her head. It was thick enough to build up some body heat beneath but too thin to settle into a deep and careless sleep each night. "Can't we just wait for the floor alarm to sound? What's the hurry?"

"The alarm sounded twenty-five minutes ago. I'm not sure we're cut out for late-night sneaking," he said, quickly covering their devices with a pillow. He wasn't scared as much as he simply didn't feel like himself. He'd never felt weakness before. Not like this. Not throughout his whole body—red ears, weak knees, a turning stomach, and a racing mind replaying his fall in the shower over and over and over again.

"Five minutes?" she cried.

Heschel was like all the other students in nearly every way possible. However, since he and Joanna had stumbled into this secret adventure, he began to notice ever so subtle differences between himself and others like Joanna.

For instance, in moments like this, which were rare by any measure, he noticed that those students who were more like Joanna responded with a greater degree of volume, movement, and drama. A lack of self-control in a moment of surprise, he thought. At other times, when the usual routine was in full swing, he could sense a gentleness in their tone and body language. A demeanor very different from those more like himself.

Being roommates, he often saw a gentleness on full display in Joanna.

"Actually, you have four minutes," he said calmly. "I've been trying to wake you for over a minute now."

Her gentleness, however, was currently hidden behind a tsunami of panicky emotion. Blanket thrashing about as though it were a straightjacket. Hair chaotically whipping in all directions as though a storm were brewing. Five jumping jacks. Uniform ripped from the hanger in her closet, which launched like an eye-piercing projectile. Five push-ups. Black shoes, gray socks, gray towels, and mustard-yellow belt yanked and pulled. Nothing about her frantic process made sense. Five sit-ups. It seemed to him that the more distress she expressed, the longer the morning routine seemed to take.

"Heschel, we're supposed to be a team. You shouldn't have let me sleep through the alarm like that."

Heschel quietly pointed at his chest, raising one eyebrow high. Another new emotion. Defensiveness. "Wait, this is my fault you're running late?"

Her face twisted. Like that of a wild animal backed into a corner. Without another word, Heschel quietly shuffled to his closet on the other side of the room, vanishing from sight. Yet another new emotion. Relational fear.

"Cover for me, would you? I'm headed for the washroom. And can you make up my side of the room? No thanks to you, I'll barely make the line!"

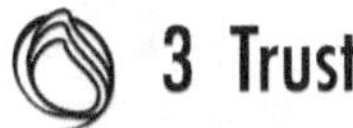

3 Trust

The cafeteria was nearly full by the time Heschel and Joanna met up. A sea of light gray uniforms with color-coded belts and respective patches on left arms signaling rank and office. Heschel, a ranking freshman, wore a yellow patch with the two white letters *W. A.* stitched with precision dead center and outlined in black thread. He had worn it proudly since the ceremony.

"How did you manage roll call?" Heschel asked with a smirk as he sat down beside her.

Joanna's cheeks flushed. "I managed it just fine, no thanks to you."

"Come on. You're not frustrated with me, are you? After

all, I'm the one a monitor almost flushed down the drain in the shower this morning."

"No, I'm not upset. It was my fault. I thought for sure a few hours of sleep would be enough. I miscalculated." Her cheeks began to glow a deeper shade of pink.

"Don't feel down. I don't blame you either. We don't know what we've gotten ourselves into."

Joanna's eyes scoured the great room. "I think we ought to keep our voices low. But not too low, or then it's obvious we're hiding something, ya know? Are you sitting on your device?"

"Yes," he said, voice crackling in a half-whisper as he felt for the tablet beneath his thigh. "Look, I'm just saying that we need a plan for when it happens."

"When what happens?" she said, taking a sip of her drink.

"You know. When one of us gets caught." His cheeks flushed at the thought of Joanna being reassigned.

"We haven't yet. And we won't if we just keep blending in." Joanna glanced around the room again.

"That might be a problem if your cheeks are going to stay red as a rose all day long," he said. Her eyes grew wide and fierce in response. Heschel immediately looked down at his tray, still full of peas and vitamin bread, peeled apple chunks, and almonds.

"Yeah, well, you wouldn't pass a fever check with all

that perspiration forming on your forehead," she shot back, quickly looking down at her half-eaten meal.

The two briefly sat in silence until Charlie sat down.

"What's up, you two? Are you sick? What's the deal with your cheeks? Want me to alert the infirmary? Is it the vitabread again?"

If anyone on Compound 40 stood out among the masses, it was Charlie. He wore the compound gray with pride. His green and blue belts were meticulously polished according to protocol. But there was something about his bouncy mannerisms that everyone knew set him apart. He was less somber than the rest of them and yet still a promising leader. Students from all four dormitories knew him and responded to him with a level of respect typically reserved for session instructors.

"Uhh, well, I was just recounting my stumble in the washroom this morning. You were there, right?" Heschel's cheeks pinked up again.

"Nope. But from what I've heard, that monitor was ready to drag you out and toss you over the edge," he said with a smirk.

"I bet the monitor is up for a promotion and doesn't want any hiccups on their record," Joanna said.

"There's something comforting about a perfect record if you ask me. Mine's pretty tight with only one year left before assignment." Charlie looked pleased with his qualifications, though his voice didn't match his demeanor.

"Where do you think you'll end up?" Heschel asked, steering away from more conversation about their strange morning.

"What if they drop you on the edge?" Joanna said, scooping peas up from her tray.

"The edge? Nah, my score's too high for that nonsense. Only a half-wit would score a patrol out there in the wastelands." Charlie paused, looked back and forth, then leaned in. "Why did you mention the edge? You know I'm overqualified for that. Did you hear about last night's breach?"

Joanna's cheeks turned crimson. Heschel began to gag.

"Heschel, are you alright?" Charlie stood up, reached over the table, and with a solid whack between the shoulder blades, Heschel coughed up a wet chunk of vitabread directly onto the center of Charlie's tray.

"Now that's disgusting," Charlie groaned. "Are you two sure there isn't something going on here?"

"Sorry...Charlie," said Heschel in between gasps. "I... thought...I saw...an...insect."

"That's it. You know I don't do bugs, and I don't do the edge. I'm gonna go find some better company."

Without another word, Charlie settled in across the hall within view. Heschel continued to clear his throat as monitors on either side of the hall looked his way. Joanna watched as one of them called in a message, presumably to the office. Seconds later, several more monitors, fully deputized, casually entered the cafeteria, settling in along the perimeter.

"Heschel?" she whispered, elbowing him in his side.

"I see them," he said, staring at his tray. "Just keep eating."

"Why are you pulling up your device?" she asked.

"Geometry," he said, tapping on his screen.

"Geometry? I'm not really interested in homework right now," said Joanna through her teeth.

"Neither am I. Do you trust me?" he said, calmly swiping at his device on the table in between them.

Joanna took a deep breath and, without missing a beat, pulled out her favorite stylus. "No, no, no!" she blurted, "You'll never get the angle right with that equation. How many times do I have to tell you that Charlie doesn't know it all?"

"You're right. You're always right, Joanna." Without prior rehearsal, the two friends put on a convincing show of faux-study. The monitors took notice and began to thin their presence in the hall.

Heschel glanced over at Charlie, who looked like he'd seen a ghost. Charlie raised an eyebrow, shrugged his shoulders, and began to mouth a question. Heschel, shaking his head as though he didn't understand, returned to his faux geometry session.

 # 4 Always Watching

Lunch had been tense, but the afternoon rolled on as usual. Rise, wash, roll call, two sessions before lunch with two more afterward, followed by dinner, evening exercises, and lights-out. The final session was divided up into two groups. The first group was formed by those who looked and functioned like Joanna. They met in the most up-to-date auditorium on the far side of Compound 40. The other group, made up of students built more like Heschel, continued to meet in the original auditorium currently under repair after a mysterious midnight electrical fire several months prior.

"I'll meet you back at the dorm after the final session,"

said Heschel. "We need to map out how we're going to inspect the artifact after lights out tonight. Have you touched it since?" Heschel covered the device attached to his wrist, hiding the camera and muffling the microphone. The tablet was clunky for a wristband, and most students didn't wear it that way, but Heschel didn't mind the bulky feel. He found it was a good way to remember that he was always connected to Stream, the communal network for the entire compound.

"I haven't been to the room since roll call, but I'm not so sure tonight's the night," she said, lowering her voice to a whisper. "Feels like I'm being watched. Why don't we give it a few days, Hesch."

Heschel didn't like the idea of waiting, but he was more intrigued by this feeling of hers. Running late, he nodded and waved as he made his way down the hall to the washroom.

Hallways were typically packed between sessions. However, the short branch dead-ending in the restroom closest to his final session remained eerily empty. That bubbly feeling in his stomach, the one he felt in the shower that morning—the one Joanna must have felt—began to stir. That's when he heard it.

"Pssst. Heschel." The hoarse whisper came from the last stall against the block wall.

"Who said that? You must be waiting for someone else.

I've got to get to the session."

"Cut it out, Heschel. Cover your device," said the familiar voice. Heschel obeyed. "What happened back there at lunch?"

"I choked on a bite of vitabread. You know how dense it is," he said, turning to leave.

"What aren't you telling me? This isn't like you." Charlie stepped out of the stall. Even with his childlike enthusiasm, he was older, taller, and all-around more mature than Heschel. "Something's changed in the last week. The last several weeks, if I'm being honest. I've never witnessed a secret scheme in action, but I imagine this is how awkward it would seem. All those stories of conspiracies put on by The Old Party. That's what this reminds me of."

Heschel's cheeks flushed red, then pink, and then a pale, dead-flesh sort of cream. Neither he nor Charlie knew anything about The Old Party other than their total despotic opposition to the Anti-Libertas leadership running Compound 40. Clutching his stomach, he folded over. The thought of being tied to The Old Party—lies and deceit and death—his stomach felt like it was going to burst.

"That's it. I'm going for the nurse."

"Don't!" growled Heschel, leaning forward on his knees, still trying to cover the device on his wrist. Charlie had never seen anyone crumble like this. Neither had Heschel, for that matter.

"Listen," said Heschel with a deep sigh. "I'm just figuring a few things out about my role here. You know what it's like to step into a higher rank. Wide Awake is an important position for someone my age. I'm just putting the pieces of my career together, that's all. You're a Fully Empowered Wide Awake. You WAFEs have it all figured out. I don't. Not yet."

Sure, Heschel used to think about his career all the time. His scores. His session seating arrangement. His monitor interaction. He used to concern himself, without emotion, of course, with the creases in his uniform and the stitching of a new patch. He used to be keenly aware of his hair length and always managed to get a trim before a monitor had to request it. He used to savor the reward of another Libertas Token in his digital wallet. He used to think clearly and appropriately, like everyone else.

Lately, however, Heschel could only think about a handful of things and all of them surrounding that object now hidden in his room. He thought about Joanna's eagerness to risk it all with him. He thought about the irony of the acronym on his arm and all the secrets and lies and curiosities now playing out in the shadows of his life. *Am I really becoming like The Old Party?*

"Your career? You're sick and flushed and off-kilter because of the patch on your shoulder?"

"I think so. Yes. Is that normal?" mumbled Heschel.

Charlie leaned back against the stall. Through the mirror, he watched his friend, now bent over and staring at the white and gray tiled floor. Charlie was sharp. He was right too. There's no way he would ever end up out on the edge with his abilities, and everyone knew it. Especially Heschel and Joanna.

"How can I help, Hesch?" His voice was earnest but professional. Two years older with patches on each shoulder and spread across his chest, there was a sense of deeper understanding about him.

"Help? I...I don't know. Do you have any advice? After all, you were in my shoes once."

"Advice?" His sigh echoed through the washroom. Heschel looked up, catching Charlie's stare in the mirror. "Truth matters. There's always a bit of grace where a secret is concerned. But truth among friends, it matters."

Heschel looked down at the floor again.

Charlie held up his device. "Always listening, Hesch," he mouthed in silence. "They're always listening." With that, he stood tall, reached down for his young friend's hand, pulled him to his feet, smoothed out the wrinkles in his uniform, then turned and left the washroom. The final session was about to begin.

Maybe Joanna is right. Tonight might not be a good night after all.

 # 5 Principal Chicanery

Attention students. The commanding voice woke them up in place of the morning alarm. Their devices came to life in unison on the charging stand with the face of Principal Chicanery staring at them—volume on high.

I see you're all awake and sitting at attention. One and the same - the same as one.

"One and the same - the same as one," repeated Heschel and Joanna, along with nearly one thousand other students across the campus. A monolith of values, beliefs, thoughts, and words. And all startled awake.

Ah yes. The sound of diversity. The sound of equitable opportunity through compliance. The sound of a generation of students who will quietly remain in their bunk while floor monitors proceed with the annual inspection. Don't move and don't worry. As one mind, we have nothing to hide from one another. I'm proud to call each one of you a stable cog in our well-oiled system. Good day.

Principal Chicanery disappeared from the screen, but neither Joanna nor Heschel moved an inch. They knew that despite their screens going dark, Chicanery was still present. Chicanery was always listening. Watching. A flushed cheek. A droplet of sweat. A nervous voice. An uncontrollable twitch. He would find what he was looking for. For the first time, this reality terrified the two of them. This power and protection used to go unnoticed, like the comfort of running water and heat. Now, however, the two remained frozen in fear at the thought.

Joanna, attempting to stretch, whispered, "I think it's a good thing we decided not to inspect the artifact this week. Things seem a bit off around here lately." Arms outstretched like wings, she gasped at the sound of the principal suddenly reappearing before them.

Oh, one more announcement. Chicanery's voice cracked like a whip in the silence. *Did I surprise you, Joanna? I suppose students have been known to squeal at my arrival.*

Her vision blurred as sweat began to form along her brow.

And you there, Heschel, are you feeling better after

your bout of stomach problems in the washroom earlier this week? I see you're still a bit flushed. Let's make an appointment to see the nurse in the infirmary, shall we?

Heschel nodded. The room began to spin. Principal Chicanery had never singled them out from the masses.

Good. We can't have our bravest and brightest Wide Awakes succumbing to infections now, can we? That's why we're here, isn't it, Heschel? That's why I am the duly elected Principal. I know what's best for each one of my students. The future class of global citizens truly set apart in body and mind for the good of the whole. Progress before people, right, Heschel?

Heschel nodded, "Yes, Principal Chicanery. Progress before people." His voice wobbled with anxiety.

One and the same - the same as one.

Once again, the screen went dark. Sweat pooled along their brows. That dark tunnel that encloses when fear grips the mind and blood floods the brain began to narrow their already blurred vision. Joanna, squinting and reaching for the wall, fell backward with a flop onto her firm pillow.

"Joanna!" Heschel cried as he hopped from his bunk. Barely out of his bed, the tunnel closed in on his sight. Without warning, he collapsed in a heap directly in front of their charging devices.

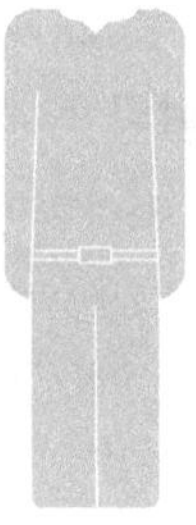

 ## 6 Breaking the Mold

Joanna, shaking herself from the stupor, rose to find Heschel in a pile of limbs and blankets on the floor. The metal nightstand next to her bed had been knocked over and was now wedged beneath his right arm and chest, propping him up and making him appear mangled and twisted. Her legs began to shake at the sight.

"Joanna?" he said in a weak voice, as though off in the distance somewhere.

"Heschel?" she replied.

"Joanna? Are you okay?" He didn't move a muscle. "Your voice is all shaky."

"Am I alright? I don't know. I'm scared to move. What if

they're watching?" she whispered, looking back and forth between their devices and her friend. "You look awful."

"We don't cry much around here, do we?" he said. He had never seen anyone cry outside of extreme physical pain. Sure, they had read about it in early biology sessions, how emotion-induced crying had once signified a key difference among peers, but that was all. They were taught nothing about the unique differences within their DNA strands or the inherently gendered makeup woven into them at birth. Hormones, estrogen, testosterone were all bypassed for the greater good. Nothing was mentioned about females and how they were more susceptible to emotional displays than males, who, on the other hand, tended to display emotion in more physically reserved ways.

Years ago, the Anti-Libertas Society had begun eliminating gendered language in education. Soon after, they successfully eliminated culturally divisive displays of emotion between men and women from the social sphere. Now, only two generations later, the Anti-Libertas appeared to have achieved their goal.

Heschel and Joanna knew they were different from one another, but what that meant in real-time, well, they had never had reason to think about it.

"Something's not right, Hesch. I'm leaking salt water from my eyes. Am I sick? I don't like it" She hesitated even to wipe the tears away, terrified at what might be happening.

"It's okay. It's something humans used to do," he said, losing steam. "I'm leaking too."

"I think we're in over our heads. And we're obviously being watched, Hesch." Joanna kept her voice low. "We've gotta get up. They'll be here any minute for inspection."

They could hear inspections taking place on either side of their room. Eyes wide with fear, Joanna jumped up like a lioness protecting her cub from a looming predator in the wilds. She wiped the salty liquid from her cheeks and quickly began inspecting the mess Heschel was in.

"There's no time, just get back in bed and pretend to sleep," said Heschel trying to sound intelligent and brave while tears began to form a pool on the floor beneath him. "There's no reason for both of us to experience re-education and reassignment. This is my mess. You know that to 'risk the loss of progress is to reap regress.'"

"I know, I know!" she shot back at him, wiping tears from her eyes. "To risk losing progress...I know, but I don't really know, ya know? I have to risk helping you. I have to risk protecting the tablet. It seems like crying and risk and fear are all tied together, and I can't stop any of it right now, and it's all very confusing."

"Okay, but they're wrapping up next door. If we're gonna do this, we've got to hurry," Heschel said while trying to move his arm.

"Honestly, how did you end up like this? What did you

trip over, Hesch?" Joanna bounced back and forth, looking for the best place to lift.

"Seriously? Do we really need to talk about how I fall over my own feet right now?" he shot back.

"On the count of three, I'll lift, and you push, and we'll drop you back onto your bunk." Joanna was feeling the power of that lioness roaring through her blood. "We can do this, Hesch!"

"One…"

"Something's gotta be broken," he wheezed.

"Two…"

"Don't grab that shoulder. Lift around my waist," he grunted.

"Three!"

"It's getting dark again! Drop me on the bed…I won't have to pretend to sleep," he said, trailing off into a whisper.

The two students gracefully swung sideways as Joanna carefully and silently guided her roommate onto his mattress without a struggle. She lifted his legs onto the bed and covered him up just as a singularly forceful knock erupted at the door.

"Inspection. On your feet," announced the monitor.

With the reflex of a wild cat, she arranged the side table while jumping into formation next to her bunk in one swift motion. Immediately four monitors strode in with precision.

Deputized inspectors? Joanna thought. *This is NOT normal. And four of them? This is a two-monitor job. At least it's always been a two-monitor job.* Joanna's mind raced with what-ifs and could-bes and 0562 and the hidden object only a few feet away.

"I said on your feet, Observer!" The lead monitor stepped toward Heschel, who appeared fast asleep in his bunk.

"That'll be enough. Leave them be." The voice came from the hall and immediately made Joanna's knees wobble. "That student has an appointment with the infirmary later today. I made it myself and will personally see to their successful recovery."

 7 Inspection

"Principal Chicanery!" Joanna caught her voice just as it began to reveal her shock. "The one who tells the truth - the truth that helps us see. Welcome to our flat, sir. It's an honor to see you in person."

"I do tend to make an impression in our Central Gatherings, don't I?" he said, stepping near and eyeing Heschel. "Needless to say, it's good to finally meet you, Joanna. I'm sorry to see your roommate here under the weather. We'll have his immune system functioning at peak prescribed condition in no time."

"Yes, Principal Chicanery. Thank you, Principal Chicanery."

"At ease, Observer," he said in a hushed voice. His tone eased her racing thoughts and yet caused her neck to stiffen. His eyes wandered around the room, pausing at blank spaces on the walls, random tiles on the floor, and finally at the stand by the door—the stand in front of the hidden hatch concealing the object.

"Joanna, are you familiar with the story behind this room?" he asked, standing with his back to her while the monitors thoroughly inspected the closets, desks, and her disheveled bed.

"No, Principal. I suppose I haven't thought much of the room." Sweat beads began to form along her hairline.

"I suppose you wouldn't have. The past isn't relevant, is it?"

"I don't know how it could be, Principal. Progress is forward, and history risks the loss of progress which only fosters regress." Talking helped calm her nerves. Programmed responses helped. Unity without emotion or thought helped. Everything about her training fostered inclusion, and this inclusion promoted obedient conformity, which carried a certain degree of mindless comfort.

"You appear to be feeling off-kilter. I don't suppose you've contracted whatever it is your roommate has come down with," said Chicanery, still looking over the stand by the door.

"Concerned, but not contracted," she confidently replied.

"Hmm," he uttered, turning towards her. "Concerned? How so?"

"Progress is made through balance. An unbalanced room fosters an inequitable future for my progress and the progress of my roommate and the progress of the entire Observer class." The words and the reasoning flowed from within. It wasn't about belief or even understanding. Growing up on Compound 40, it was all she knew. Unity meant progress. Period.

The monitors nearly dropped their devices, startled by the sudden burst of Chicanery's boisterous laugh. "My, my, my, you are a well-conditioned young student. I wonder if a new Wide Awake isn't standing before us. I may even see you assigned to Chagrin Center in little more than a few years!" His laugh broke out in uncontrolled bursts as the monitors attempted their routine, breaking from their stride with each untimely howl.

"Yes, Principal Chicanery. Thank you, Principal Chicanery."

"We truly have streamlined the process, haven't we?" he said under his breath. "It's a wonder that it happened so quickly. It always happens so quickly, you know? Like a tide that rises slowly at first and then all of a sudden, you're caught up in the undertow, helpless and unaware of any way out. The other compounds, well, they drowned. But this one? This time? I do believe we've caught the tide."

The room grew silent as the principal resolved his odd musings.

"Principal Chicanery, the room is clean," said the lead monitor. "I'll personally sign off on this one unless you have something to add."

"Sign off, sign off. We're set here. This room has a history, though it appears that line might finally be breaking. Never without a few hiccups, I suppose." With a gentle nod toward Joanna, he turned and left the room. The monitors followed suit, closing the door as they went.

Oh Heschel, what are we going to do? Joanna thought, staring at the secret cubby.

8 The Return

It had been two weeks since Heschel's visit to the infirmary. He was different. Not oblivious to Joanna and her questions. Not ignorant of the circumstances that put them in this odd position. But not yet directly acknowledging the ordeal either. The new emotions were gone, or at least suppressed, along with all haste for discovery. In place of it all, however, grew a greater awareness of surveillance across Compound 40. For the most part, he simply began acting in his official capacity as a Wide Awake, or so it seemed to Joanna and Charlie.

"You're staring at your vitabread again," said Heschel, gently elbowing Joanna in the ribs.

"Wait, what? Did you say something?" she replied, blinking and shaking her head.

"Where were you just now?" he said, with a tone that seemed too impersonal for Joanna to take seriously.

"Where am I?" she said, raising her voice. "Don't clear your throat at me. I've been here this whole time waiting for you to wake up from whatever happened to you in the infirmary!"

"Whoops! Would you look at that? I just spilled my nutrient-rich goat milk smoothie all over the table. Now it's running onto the floor." Bending over with his napkin to clean it up, he grabbed Joanna's wrist, pulling her down to the ground. "Grab a napkin, would you? And leave your device on the table. Wouldn't want it to get covered in smoothie."

"What are you doing?" she growled.

"Calm down! You can't just go and lose all self-control in the middle of a crowded room. You're going to get yourself an appointment in the infirmary, and believe me... they won't take it easy on you. Not after that morning."

"So you do remember!" she said, throwing her hand over her mouth to stifle her excitement.

"Of course I do. And so do they. Every monitor here is tasked with keeping an eye on our every move. I'd be surprised if this little stunt doesn't send me back for round two."

"Round two of what? What happened in there?"

"Now's not the time. But if we make it through the day, I'll tell you all about it tonight after lights out. But you have to hold it together. Do you hear me? No matter what happens, remember, one and the same - the same as one."

She nodded.

"I hear the monitors marching. Stay calm."

Heschel began crawling out from beneath the table when he heard a voice intervene from behind.

"Excuse me, monitors, my name is Charlie, WAFE Interpreter," he said in a gentle, professional voice. "I sincerely apologize for interrupting your movement, but I'd hate for you to interrupt the current social experiment I've devised that's taking place directly behind me."

"Explain yourself, Interpreter," said the monitor in the lead, hand on taser, ignoring the beeping coming from their device.

"Of course," he continued, clearing his throat. "You see, these two are hopeful prospects. One more than the other, if you know what I mean. I've designed a series of seemingly random events intended to cause stress through unnecessary attention," he said, leaning in with a whisper, "you know, to see how future leaders might respond to peers during unexpected events."

"You spilled the drink at that table?" asked the monitor sternly.

"I suppose you're skeptical. Rightly so. Needless to say, I devised it with the hopes of weeding out the weaker one to focus my training more equitably among the one who deserves it. Progress before people, correct?"

Heschel stayed low. Very low. He had managed to slowly crawl to the other side of the table, peering through the cracks at the interaction unfolding.

"What on the edge is he up to?" Joanna whispered.

"I don't know, but something in my gut tells me things just got a little more confusing," said Heschel.

Joanna shook her head in disbelief. Her code-length hair stuck to her forehead as she calmly sloshed the spilled liquid back and forth with her saturated napkin. Each student was allowed one cloth napkin per meal. They were hardly absorbent, made of rough linen, the same as their uniform. And drab gray, too. "Austerity symbolizes prosperity," or so the old saying went. Meager resources meant safety, security, and most of all, progress.

Heschel watched the monitor nod, silence their device, and disperse with the others in tow. He watched the matte black leather of Charlie's session shoes as they turned and leisurely strolled in his direction. He paused in unison with the shoes as they stopped directly beside him.

"Young Observers, Heschel and Joanna, may I have a word with you?" he said, loud enough for all to hear.

As though being summoned by The Head of the Chamber

of Trust, Heschel and Joanna dropped their wet napkins, rose to their feet, and silently stood in formation—arms behind their backs, hands gripped, necks stiff, backs straight, feet shoulder-width apart—facing Charlie.

"As the ranking WAFE in your dorm, I would like to have a private word with you two about this little experiment I've conducted," he said, without a hint of friendship. Not angry or formidable or accusatory, but professional, as though they had never personally interacted before.

The two young students nodded compliantly.

"Good. Now retrieve the proper cleaning materials from the resource office and do this floor justice. I want all students who sit in this section from now on to experience a floor so clean that they too will be inspired to bring a renewed sense of pride to their work here on our majestic compound," he said, with a natural air of authority about him. "I'll make it a point to visit your flat this evening after all activities have concluded for the day to debrief. Are we clear?"

The two young students nodded again.

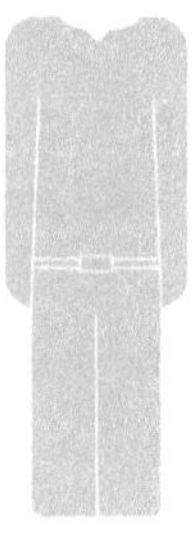

 **9 It's Time**

"Is he with us or against us, Hesch?" whispered Joanna, laying across her bed with a book covering her mouth in view of their devices charging on the wall.

"He made it a point to remind me that I'm always in their sight as if I didn't know," he responded, sitting on the floor and facing away from digital eyes. "Everyone knows they're always watching. Every student here knows that. Why use it as a threat?"

"Because you don't just know it now, you're aware of it," she said. "So, when you were strapped to the table, did the nurse inject you with anything, or was it all cognitive influence?"

"No injections. No chemicals, vaccines, or psychedelics. Just a continuous loop of Anti-Libertas leaders discussing how the Safe Space came to be." Heschel stared at the floor as he spoke. His voice was soft, the kind of soft you can only hear after laying in bed for half an hour in the silence of the night.

"Was it like The Chamber's Critical-History sessions played in successive order? You know, like a timeline on repeat?" asked Joanna, trying to imagine the scene.

"Sort of, I suppose," he mumbled, still trying to make sense of it. "There were session clips for sure, but then there were all these old-looking clips of people I've never heard of or seen before. And they were so…I don't know… vitriolic and demanding and demeaning. And what they were saying didn't really make any sense. They didn't seem to fit with the rest of the video."

"Like what?" she pushed, hungry for more detail.

"I only remember a couple of phrases," he said, staring off as though watching a screen replay the images of angry people dressed in strange clothes, clothes that seemed to fit their personalities and profiles. "An angry individual with shiny beads in their hair standing, shouting at an audience, 'Our families need to be deconstructed, reshaped, and redefined! The angry Christian patriarch needs to be torn down once and for all!'" he paused again. "There's so much in there that doesn't make sense."

"Christian? Is that some sort of ancient tribe? But there's the family idea again, like 0561 said, remember? Reshaping the family tradition. And what's a patriarch? And why would it need to be torn down?" Joanna rolled onto her back, gazing at the pages overhead while trying to imagine what these words, these ideas, could mean.

"There's a senior character too," he said, turning to face her. "A leader, I suppose. Bright white hair, geriatric in all their mannerisms though not so angry, really, only poking at people, like you would the opposite team in a training exercise to rile them up a bit. Poking with an air of arrogance. 'There is absolutely no difference whatsoever between a man and a woman. The sciences have spoken, and don't let anyone tell you otherwise!'" Heschel leaned back, his eyes shifting. "What does that even mean? And why show me those clips?"

"What's a *man*? Sounds connected to hu-man," said Joanna, as though discussing some sort of undiscovered alien creature.

"What's a *wo-man?*" Heschel shot back. "I'm not sure, but I'm guessing they were in those strange clothes in the clips? Gowns and woven jackets with buttons and collars and shiny gold chains hanging from their ears. I mean, their features looked different, but so do yours and mine."

"I wonder if that's what they call brainwashing?" she thought out loud.

"Brainwashing?"

"You sound surprised," she said. "Come on, Heschel. What else would you call being strapped down and forced to mentally absorb one version of history, a story we obviously know nothing about, by the way, until your mind washes clean of our discoveries?"

"I don't know. Mind-scrub sounds better." Joanna sighed, and the two sat in silence as the sun fell beyond the edge. He remembered something else about the re-education process, something he couldn't even begin to explain. A hushed voice with an air of confidence came and went throughout the process. It didn't overcome the reprogramming or drown out the noise. And it didn't come through the headphones. It was deeper than that. It seemed to resonate from below it all. Foundational. The source of something more powerful and earnest than The Chamber. And it was comforting beyond anything he'd ever felt in his entire life.

Charlie would arrive any minute, and neither Heschel nor Joanna had any idea what to expect. The main light in their room was off, and it grew dark quickly. The lights-out buzzer sounded throughout the floor.

"It's been fifteen minutes, and I haven't heard a peep in the hall," said Joanna, hoping Charlie had forgotten about their meeting.

"I think we should inspect the item."

This was the first time Heschel mentioned anything of their find since the infirmary.

"What if he shows up?" Joanna shot back in a hoarse whisper.

"I have this feeling in my gut that it's going to be alright if he does."

"A feeling in your gut?" Joanna chuckled. "What on the edge is that supposed to mean?"

"I don't know how to explain it," he said, feeling his cheeks flush again. "I think it's connected to all those emotions we've been overcome by in the past few weeks. Fear and anxiety and anger and confusion and compassion. Things that make blood rush to our cheeks as it courses its way to the brain before making sense of it."

"A gut feeling," she repeated under her breath.

"A gut feeling."

"Well, I wasn't sure when you'd be ready, if ever, after your trip, so I've been taking cleaning wipes from the maintenance cart in passing. One at a time," she said with a smirk. "I figured we'd need something disposable to study the relic properly."

Heschel smiled. She was more courageous than she gave herself credit for.

Without another word, Joanna made her way to the small stand by the door. It was short, about thigh-high, with a solid back to it. Large enough to set books on when entering the room after the session. Without making a sound, she slid it away from the wall while still blocking the view of the overseeing devices on the charging station directly across the room.

"Here's the deal," she said. "Fifteen minutes and not a second more. If the monitors in rotation are spying on us, then at most, we'll have a ten-minute window before they cycle through each of the floors before returning to us. Five minutes more, and the monitors will be pounding on the door. On my count, cover those devices."

"Look, we'll have to remember everything we see—no devices for storing private files. We can't afford a digital paper trail," Heschel said, as though having practiced this safety protocol. "I'll focus on the words. You focus on everything else."

"Wait for the minute to turn over, and we'll get started," Joanna said, staring directly at the clock on her tablet. "Three...two...one...cover them."

A gentle knock at the door made Joanna squeal like a mouse caught in a trap.

 # 10 Charlie Arrives

"**W**hat do we do?" Joanna said, choking on her squeal.

"We open the door," said Heschel, adjusting his uniform and sitting a bit taller.

It wasn't a long pause, but Joanna could feel the tension rise as her cheeks blushed. Thankfully it was dark, so she didn't have to explain her wincing as the unease of letting Charlie in on their discovery began to ache in her chest.

"It's not just a gut feeling, you know," he said. "It's years of watching Charlie treat others with genuine respect that other students only offer systematically. It's the odd warning in the washroom. It's the strange cover-up in the cafeteria."

With a deep breath and a long sigh that eased the swelling anxiety like a release valve on a pressure cooker, Joanna calmly rose to her feet and opened the door. There were no locks to unlock or deadbolts to turn. After all, who was there to fear when all thoughts and actions were unified? What privacy was possible when all devices were readily available behind closed doors? What was there to protect when all property belonged to The Chamber?

The hallway light shone directly upon Heschel, illuminating the object in his hands. Charlie quickly stepped into the dark room, swiftly closing the door behind him. Motioning to the two of them not to say a word, he pointed to the floor, and in unison, they sat down in a semicircle.

Staring at the dark, ancient object between them, he bluntly asked, "Can I hold it?"

Joanna and Heschel looked at one another. She nodded, and Heschel, without hesitation, handed him the stone. It measured nearly six inches wide, with the broken edge spanning almost eight inches. The stone was less than an inch thick and caked in hardened clay.

"It's heavy," Charlie said. "I didn't expect that. I guess I didn't know what to expect tonight."

"I think it's a type of dark granite," said Heschel. "Geology isn't my thing, but it seems strong and workable enough to chisel by hand, you know?"

"It's incredibly shiny after all this time. At least the part not covered in clay," said Charlie, tracing the lines with his finger. "But it's not granite. It's onyx. Black onyx. And these cuts are too perfect to have been done by hand."

"It's just how it was when we found it," said Joanna, nearly forgetting that Charlie might be spying on them. "Tonight's the first night we're chancing a short investigation."

Charlie flashed a look at Heschel. "Feels like symbols in a pattern," he noted under his breath.

"Pictures? Characters maybe? A secret code?" wondered Heschel. "We haven't done an ounce of research on it."

"Don't record it," Charlie shot back.

"In the mind," the two responded in chorus.

"In the mind only," continued Joanna. "We can't afford a digital trail of notes. In fact, after we turn on the spotlight, we're estimating fifteen minutes of inspection at most. Probably less now that you're here. No doubt they're tracking your visit."

They could hear the wind pick up outside, whistling across the window screen just as a light flashed across the glass from below—a monitor making their usual rounds.

"Ten minutes at best," Charlie uttered in a rushed whisper. "You know, they've asked me to keep an eye on you two. Principal Chicanery himself asked me to take you under my wing, Joanna. And to keep you in line, Hesch. So yes, they're tracking me."

The two flashed looks of fear at one another. Enough light emanated through the cracks of the door that they could read each other's expressions. After a short, heavy pause, Heschel broke the silence. "Ten minutes," he whispered.

"Ten minutes beginning at 9:30," said Joanna, taking hold of the stone and handing it back to Heschel. "He risked his life on the edge to pull it from the earth. He gets first go of it."

"What do you imagine it says?" asked Charlie. "It's old, but it seems mostly decorative. I can't imagine you'd have found anything too ancient on these grounds. It did manage to survive the purge all those years ago, so maybe someone wanted it to be found."

"Remember that session when we were young, about ancient relics? Objects created by tribes wasting resources on forms of art intended to make leaders and groups feel special and maintain power," said Joanna.

"Yeah, like mythological symbols of worship before The Chamber of Trust streamlined reality. Before they distinguished universal truth from tribal lies, myths, and alternate worldviews," Heschel added, gently snapping off dried clay chunks covering the stone. Fifteen more seconds before switching on the spotlight.

"What's your point?" said Charlie.

"Well, I don't know. It's just that, ever since Joanna and

I started down this path of discovering the truth behind all of our education under The Chamber, well, it makes me wonder if these old relics might not tell another side of our history."

"Are you saying that our history might not be a *true* and *total* history of it all?" Charlie asked with a hint of humor in his voice. "Are you questioning The Chamber's motives?"

"Well, yeah," said Joanna, the weight of her claim hitting her. "Someone started this project before us. They hid items in this secret compartment behind the table. Items that led us to the waterfall. And The Chamber said these old relics were either a myth or were destroyed by their people when they woke up to the Anti-Libertas' reality. And Heschel's brainwashing experience in the infirmary. And that monitor reassigned after mentioning an old family tradition."

"Sssshhhhhhhh!" Charlie threw a hand over each of their mouths. "You absolutely cannot ever repeat that list of oddities. Do you hear me? Never." All three nodded in agreement as the clock struck 9:30. "There are too many eyes and ears around here."

"Hit the flashlight," said Heschel, shaking off Charlie's hand. "Let's not waste a second."

With the object held tight, the others huddled around Heschel, observing, watching, noting, and waiting for their turn. Three minutes each, with the final minute on the floor between them. Heschel observed the symbols. Joanna studied the dimensions, the shape, and the broken edge. Now that Charlie was involved in sharing the mental load, he took the role of reviewing the stone tablet's features in general, like a catch-all or an understudy. The more eyes and minds, the more they'd likely uncover.

The dorm was quiet. It was always quiet. No student ever stayed out too late, nor did they ever wake up too early. Structure was safety, and safety was defined by The Chamber. The three worked in absolute silence: feeling, cleaning, repeating, memorizing, passing.

"That's it," said Joanna. "Times up." She immediately returned the stone to its secret cubby before turning off the flashlight.

"Any thoughts on the characters?" asked Heschel, sitting in near-total darkness with only a little moonlight glowing beyond the window.

"Yeah, but I'll need to do a little research to flesh them out a bit. No doubt the symbols and shapes are Ancient Mesopotamian or some sort of Middle Eastern," Charlie said, letting the magnitude of the deception settle in.

"Time's up, you two," Joanna cut in. "You can hear the monitors moving in the far stairwell, can't you?"

They rose to their feet, and Charlie leaned in. "I want to see the location where you found this. I don't believe it's an accident that this survived. The other half is out there, and it's gonna be key to our understanding." Without another word, Charlie slipped out of the room. Joanna and Heschel relaxed, uncovered their devices, then settled into their separate bunks for the night.

 **11 The Sojourn**

Two weeks had passed since that night inspecting the object. All three agreed not to discuss their observations until the end of the month when the quarterly Sojourn would give them cover. The fall weather had arrived just in time for the adventure. The Sojourn was a four-day role-playing survival game held each season in which students were encouraged to team up in groups of two to four. Each team would work to bolster their self-worth, reputation, and communal rank through successful preparation and survival from the inevitable attack of the Deplorables—a common yet unrealized threat woven into their education by The Chamber. Each day teams would be mentally, emotionally, and physically challenged by monitors, who, like the students, were endlessly vying for notability among the zealously obedient.

"Are you two ready to survive all the wild perils The Chamber has to throw at us this weekend?" asked Charlie.

"I've never actually participated in The Sojourn," said Joanna.

"Wait, what's that?" he replied, dropping the supplies he had been strategically organizing for their secret mission that very night. "So you've only been part of the Remnant? Really? I mean, you're obviously willing to take on a challenge or two." Charlie was a multi-year veteran who had placed on the podium each quarter since he was first eligible to participate at age ten. "After all, you're the main reason they sent me to keep a close eye on you two."

Joanna fumbled with her supplies for a moment, losing focus on their purpose and placement. It was still a sobering reality to think Charlie was commissioned to spy on them. Sure, they were always connected to Stream via devices that were always listening, watching, and communicating their actions, but this was an invasive way to control a student. And it was unnerving.

"It just seems wrong to pit one student against another," she said, at last, tossing her supplies on the table. "One and the same - the same as one, right?"

Heschel felt the same, though he had already concluded

that life on Compound 40, maybe even life as a whole, was not quite as straightforward as what The Chamber had taught them.

Charlie shoved his device into the rolled-up blanket inside his pack. "I don't know if charging me to spy is being one and the same or not. We're students. You're Observers, and I'm an Interpreter. We're only beginning to understand the bigger picture through our sessions. And now this discovery? It *seems* life-changing, but did you ever think that maybe we're being shielded from something much worse out there beyond the edge? That maybe the Deplorables are more deplorable than we could ever imagine? Or that some historical data just isn't safe?"

Charlie popped up from his perch on the table next to Joanna just as a troop of monitors cut through the cafeteria now used as a supply station for The Sojourn. About fifty students, one-fifth of their dorm, would be testing their survival skills. The rest, the Remnant, would remain within the parameters of their buildings, free to use their time as they pleased, though most would spend it watching The Sojourn live on Stream while rooting for their flat-mates, age brackets, and dorms in general.

Though Heschel was more paranoid about the monitors' whereabouts since his time in the infirmary, he readily admitted that there was no discernable deviation in their movements or interactions with him. They must have known that he was in on Principal Chicanery's plans and made the extra effort not to give away the plot. He reasoned that Charlie was the cause for their lack of interest.

"Here's the deal," said Heschel, "we're packing for two separate events. First, The Sojourn, which we'll have to participate in just enough to be taken seriously."

"And the secret sojourn," whispered Joanna. "I know, Heschel. We've got it covered."

"Repetition is the tool for reformation through and through," Heschel poetically recited.

"Seriously? I haven't heard that one since I was a Seeker, Hesch!" Charlie's laugh caught the attention of all the students throughout the cafeteria. Laughter wasn't an odd sound around the grounds. However, there were certain laughs—uncontrollably robust laughs—sort of like Charlie's outburst that were associated with a lack of discipline. And discipline was key to order on the compound.

With a gruff whisper, Joanna snapped, "That's enough, you two! Seriously. I don't know what it is, but your kind always manages to get sidetracked with the simplest comments, tasks, or observations. It's almost like, I don't know, like your maturity regresses for a moment." She looked around the room, confirming that all extra eyes and ears had resumed their tasks before saying another word. "I don't know what it is, but you two think too much alike. You're just different from me and my kind in the strangest ways. I don't get it."

Heschel and Charlie looked at one another and smirked. They knew she was right, but like her, they couldn't quite put their finger on what was actually different between them.

"I'm all set," Charlie said with excitement. "I'm gonna head up to my room and finish preparations. I'll meet you two in the sojourner's circle this afternoon."

After Charlie had left, along with most of the other students, Joanna melted into a seat at the table. Staring out the window, she watched the trees sway in the wind, something she was prone to do in her room from time to time.

"We're going to be okay, you know," Heschel said, gently sinking in beside her.

"You know that gut feeling we've been noticing more and more this past month or so?"

"Yeah, are you feeling it too?"

Placing her hands on her stomach, she nodded. "You feel it? Cause you're not acting like it."

"Yeah, I still don't know what it is, though," he said, sighing deeply. "It's different from what I felt the day I passed out in our room or when Charlie cornered me in the washroom. And while I was scared at first in the re-education center, that fear shifted to a sort of fluid calmness I can't really explain. This feels a little like that."

"What do you think it is?"

"A pull."

"A pull?" whispered Joanna, squinting as she watched the trees sway.

"Something pulling or maybe pushing me, us, to keep going—to pursue the truth."

"I feel that too," she said, arms crossed and tight. "Yet still nervous."

 # 12 The Sojourner's Circle

The circle was packed. Nearly 175 students squeezed in tight this year, buzzing with anticipation. Students from all four dorms made up of teams ages ten and up were crammed into a space designed for a comfortable crowd of 100 or so.

The youngest teams stood in the front, with the older students crammed in all around. While the excitement built and typically burst with the call to action, there remained a high level of self-control. Of course, The Chamber commanded a high degree of order, but it also fostered a healthy dose of fear during The Sojourn. Heschel hadn't noticed it before. Neither had Charlie. Fear of failure, personal as well as collective. Fear of the monitors and the challenges they might release. Fear of the compound at night and the ever warned-against Deplorables. Fear of Principle Chicanery.

That last one hit Heschel especially hard. His time in the infirmary and the knowledge of Charlie's secret assignment by Chicanery himself, well, this reality check brought clarity to a fear he hadn't recognized in the past. A fear subversively projected from the top down and worked into every ounce of training he could recall.

Charlie wormed his way through the crowd toward his teammates at the center of the circle. Being a popular leader, it seemed everyone wanted a piece of him, both in person and on Stream.

"Good luck, Charlie!"

"See you in the winner's circle!"

"You're spot's mine this year, Charlie. Winner takes all!"

"Partnered up with some green fish this fall, eh Charlie?"

"Hope you make it through the first round, Charlie!"

By the time he caught up with them, he was pretty hyped. On the other hand, Joanna looked as though she were attending the calling hours of an old deceased acquaintance. Not sad, but solemn. Heschel stood motionless, eyeing each monitor standing firm around the perimeter, now waiting for the initial charge.

"Can you feel it?" said Charlie. "That surge of energy

welling up for survival? Every Sojourn, it strikes me how much we're wired for this type of inevitable action. It's who we are, our species, you know?"

He wasn't really talking to them. He was a leader, trained in the ideology of The Chamber, and despite their newfound discoveries, he was still very much a product of the Anti-Libertas school. He was smacking Heschel's back and high-fiving other teams when she walked up.

She was short with straight, dark black hair and carrying a full pack as though ready for The Sojourn, yet frantic as she grasped for Charlie's attention.

"Charlie!" she yelled, drowned out by the chants and cheers. "Charlie!"

Charlie whipped around in all directions looking over her head with each pass. "Seems everyone is reaching out for a piece of me. Relax, I've got time for everyone!" he said to no one in particular.

Joanna didn't recognize her, but it was a large compound after all. Tapping her on the shoulder, she asked, "Hey, are you alright?"

"Not really," said the girl, restrained yet panicky. "I need to talk to Charlie. He'll know what to do."

"Here's how you do it," said Joanna as she turned towards Charlie, held her hand up for a high-five, and then grabbed hold of his when he smacked it.

"Charlie, this student wants to speak with you."

"Oh, so you're the one tugging on my uniform," he said with a smile. "Wait, what's wrong?"

"I...well, you see...it's just that..." she closed her eyes and took a deep breath. "Charlie, my team came down with a stomach virus and had to drop out of The Sojourn. I need a team, and I can't find anyone in my age group with an open spot. Do you know anyone with space for another member?"

"Charlie, are you okay? You look frightened," she said, stepping back slowly.

"Um, yeah…I mean, no…I'm fine," he mumbled, making eye contact with Joanna and Heschel, both of whom looked their own version of terrified. "To be honest, I don't know of any team with an open spot either. It's pretty packed this fall, you know. It's the big one before winter sets in. Let's try again next spring, okay?"

"Charlie, I'm not like you," she pleaded. "I'm sure to be assigned to menial tasks, not that there's anything wrong with that, but I'd really like to try and earn some self-worth points for a better assignment, you know? I don't have to win. Just help out with a team. I'll stay out of the way."

Her face remained steadfast without emotion though her voice shook when she spoke. Most students would end up with general assignments: laundry, groundskeeping, food service, transportation—and these were all noble tasks, necessary jobs for the good of The Chamber, but even students with mild mannerisms and gentle natures initially hold to the idea of more significant assignments and agency within or beyond Compound 40.

"We have an open spot." The words seemed to fall out of Joanna's mouth.

Heschel and Charlie didn't move a muscle.

"I understand," Joanna said. "This is my first Sojourn too. You can join us. It's just the three of us, after all." Silence. "What do you say, Hesch?"

Heschel stood motionless.

"That's a great idea, Joanna!" said Charlie, breaking the pause with his diplomatically upbeat voice. "Why didn't I think of that? We'd love to have you, and we'll be better off for it!"

Charlie stared at Heschel. The kind of stare that speaks a bookful of information through the dilation of the pupils.

"Absolutely!" Heschel said with a forced smile. "What's your name? Age? Dorm?"

"Maria," she said with pursed lips and closed eyes, gently shaking her head in disbelief. "Thank you so much! I won't let you down. I'm an Observer. I'm in the Eastern Dorm, same as you three."

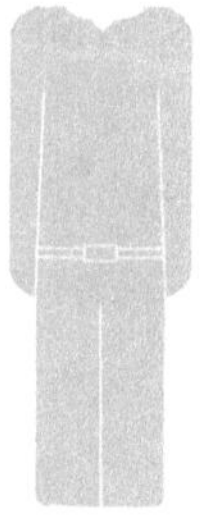

 # 13 The Czar Speaks

The crowd erupted as Principal Chicanery took the stage.

Every device in the circle flashed and chimed as Stream broadcasted his arrival. Students of all ages lifted their tablets high, shouting, "One and the same - the same as one! One and the same - the same as one!"

Heschel and Joanna stood behind Charlie and Maria, watching as they, too, raised their devices high, chanting the Anti-Libertas mantra. The two looked at one another, nodded, then slowly lifted their devices into the air with the rest of the crowd.

Welcome to the infamous fall Sojourn!

The circle was located in front of the main building and

flanked by dorms on either side. His voice echoed off of The Adavis Center for Progress directly behind them. The infirmary, which housed the re-education room, was deep within the Adavis building. Heschel hadn't taken notice of the building before or committed much emotion to his awful experience in the infirmary, but now, staring at Principal Chicanery with the center haunting from behind, he felt boxed in. But he also felt a renewed sense of commitment deep inside to the mission at hand.

"I'm not going back," he said in a hushed voice to Joanna as they stood there, arms held high.

"To the infirmary?"

"To any of it!" His teeth clenched tight. "This Sojourn is going to change things. I can feel it."

Maria looked back at the two of them standing there with devices half-heartedly swaying in the air offbeat with the rest of the crowd. She smiled an equally half-hearted smile then quickly looked forward obediently.

You are gearing up to embark on one of the year's most engaging challenges. The fall challenge is always a special one for me. It's when I discovered I had what it takes to activate fellow students!

The crowd cheered.

To socially engineer change among my peers for the greater good!

Students waved their devices wildly above their heads.

To tear down another layer of that old broken system and turn it into who we are today!

The swelling cheers rolled like waves along the shore.

"I heard something else while I was strapped face-down in that windowless room," said Heschel, device slowly lowering.

Joanna leaned in.

"I didn't want to say anything before. It seemed so strange when it happened, but all of this is strange, and it's the truth, right? The truth didn't use to sound strange, or at least what we always thought was the truth, but now the real truth, this new truth we're digging up, it almost feels wrong not to say it out loud. It's like I have to share it no matter how ridiculous it might sound," he said, stamping his feet and smacking himself across the cheek before thrusting his device back toward the sky to join the hovering flock of glowing tablets.

Joanna stood still, eyes wide, leaning in.

It was in that Sojourn fifty years ago today that the Anti-Libertas movement found their most aggressive leader!

The crowd began to bounce like ripples across a too-small pond, ready to burst beyond the edges.

A czar of ingenuity!

The ripples grew into waves.

A micro-aggravator fully woke and willing to snatch control from those myth-masters, those zealots, those barbaric Deplorables—whatever the human toll! Whatever the social unrest! Whatever the financial cost! A sacrifice by me is a sacrifice for all!

Bodies were bouncing and bumping around the still-island of Heschel and Joanna wedged into the center of it all.

"A quiet voice," he said, drawing close to her. "A whisper like a soothing wind in the middle of the mental chaos. A voice I'd never heard before. An indescribable calm."

"What did it say?"

And now it's your turn. One of you will soon be primed to take my place. To build on these traditions. To solidify The Chamber's truth once and for all by weeding out those malfunctioning few who stumble and wander and conspire. I can hardly wait to see you all back here in the sojourner's circle, ready to reward the winning team with the honor they deserve.

The crowd cheered like never before. "One and the same - the same as one! One and the same - the same as one! One and the same - the same as one!"

"'I am in you, and you are in me,'" recited Heschel with an unnatural air of calm in his voice. A calmness made all the more distinct amid the raucous mob.

"Heschel, your arm! You dropped your arm! Raise it! Raise it up!" cried Joanna, cutting through the deafening chants. Before he could shake off his bout of wanderlust, the devices of all those students within a five-foot circumference of him began to vibrate, flash red and white, and sound a horrifyingly shrill alarm. Heschel's device, however, flashed a golden sun of a yellow, and just as blindingly bright, with a siren wail to match.

The mob came to an immediate standstill. All eyes locked onto the radiant sun. Heschel's eyes, however, shot toward the stage, directly meeting Principal Chicanery's eyes dead-on.

Well, now, if it isn't one of the very students I was referring to.

 14 Heschel's Reply

Young Observer Heschel. How are we feeling today at the start of the fall Sojourn?

His sensation of peace? Gone. So startling was the transition from reimagining that gentle voice in the barrage to this chaotic state of anxiety under the watchful eye of Principal Chicanery and all of his peers that Heschel instantly regretted having ever felt these new emotions.

"Principal Chicanery," he said, choking out the best imitation of Charlie's diplomatic voice he could muster.

Well, student, you're either under the weather again or excited beyond bodily control. Which is it, I wonder?

Heschel felt the crowd pressing in. Those familiar faces

and eyes seemed to warp and twist at the shriek of the alarm. He could feel his blood begin to thump throughout his limbs. Each vein expanding and every nerve tingling. His knees wobbled while his cheeks grew red as Gala apples ripe for the picking. Joanna stood by, helpless.

"Principal Chicanery," he said, once again, now searching the crowd as one clamoring for a lifeboat in a raging ocean and reaching for guidance, direction, safety.

Joanna, unnoticed by her peers, scooched nearer to her friend. Sensing her presence Heschel stood taller, his lips pursed and his knees beginning to bounce with adrenaline.

"Principal Chicanery," he called out again, with the bold voice of a future victor. "I couldn't be feeling any better if you dropped me into a circle of Deplorables, turned out the lights, and told me to end their ignorant suffering. Let The Sojourn begin!"

The crowd gasped while turning toward the stage for permission to respond. Principal Chicanery stared at the two of them. Was he aware of their impending midnight excursion? Did he know of the stone relic? Is it possible that he was aware of the voice beneath the noise? Whatever his reason for the long pause, he refused to disappoint this youthful mob for anything in the world—especially not today of all days.

Young Observer, you're the model student. Yes, the perfect specimen of confidence and conviction. Monitors,

Charlie grabbed hold of Heschel's shoulders, jumping and shaking as the mob cheered in a whirlwind of excitement. Securing gear, giving high fives, and, like cattle, working their way out of the circle through a narrow pass formed by dozens of deputized monitors, the mass of students rushed into the wilds like an escaping herd before the round-up. Heschel turned and nodded at Charlie and Maria. The four of them picked up their gear and melted into the exodus. As they funneled through the monitors, shoulder to shoulder, Heschel flashed a subtle smile at Joanna. They had survived the first challenge.

The second challenge of the night? Adjust their plans to accommodate the newest member of the team.

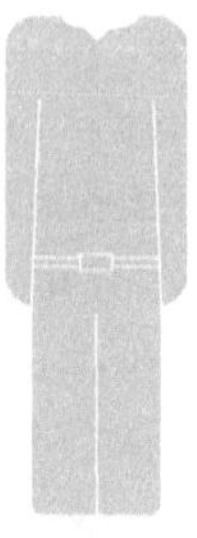

 # 15 Basecamp

"**W**hy are we heading straight toward the waterfall?" asked Joanna. "Won't that be too obvious?"

"Why would that be obvious?" asked Maria. "Do a lot of students camp there?"

Charlie smiled then ran ahead with Heschel to conjure up some new plans now that Maria had joined the fold.

"I guess I was just thinking that running water is freshwater and that a lot of teams might want to be as close to it as possible." Joanna was beginning to feel a slight pressure in her chest. She wasn't sure what to make of all these new feelings—anxiety, excitement, fear, compassion—rising and subsiding every day. She had never experienced the compounding toll that lying has on every inch of a person's being—heart, mind, body, and whatever this otherworldly feeling was. She had never even considered conjuring up a lie before all this began.

"I didn't know there was a waterfall on the compound," Maria said. "It must be pretty far out along the edge."

"Yep, quite a ways out too. Let's catch up and see what the plan is," she said, trying to change the subject and avoid the weight of more lies.

"Have you been out there?"

"Well...yeah...once."

"Why? I thought you'd never competed in The Sojourn before?" Maria's questions had no emotion in them, simply those of a student seeking data. Normal. However, Joanna didn't like the questions. More questions meant more lying.

"Well, I've become more and more interested in geography. More than other students, I suppose," she said, feeling the weight lift as truth began to weave its way back into her conversation. "It's a recent discovery. In fact, had you asked me that a few months ago, I wouldn't have known anything more than the rest, just a river winding its way through Compound 40 along the edge and into the wilds."

"So, where do you think Charlie is leading us?" Maria asked, content with Joanna's answer.

Joanna shrugged her shoulders, picked up her pace, and

waved Maria on to catch up with the other half of the team.

It was late in the year, and the sun would be down soon without much warning. They needed to set up camp, begin dinner preparations, and put two synchronized plans into action—one for The Sojourn and the other for what felt like a budding disaster.

Other teams heading in the same direction thinned out sporadically, setting up camp along the way. They ran until they alone found their way further along the edge and inevitably toward the waterfall.

"I'll prep the meal," said Charlie, controlled and confident.

"I'll collect wood for the fire," Maria offered, already on her way to gather some kindling.

"We'll keep it light tonight—vitabread from our stash, and I know of a patch of rhubarb growing just beyond the treeline," Charlie continued. "We'll boil some water, maybe a little lemongrass-mint tea for a kick. That stuff grows all over down here." Pointing toward Heschel and Joanna, "You two set up the tents."

"Sounds good."

They raised the tents to face one another on the fire's north side. A tarp, fastened in the space above both entrances, dropped down the north side to create both a shelter from the oncoming rain and a wall to block inevitable spying eyes from meetings around the fire pit. Angled slightly in a V-pattern, they managed to cover more than half of their campsite.

"Heschel!" cheered Charlie. "This is an incredible blockade. Nicely done!"

"Thank Joanna," he said. "She may not have Sojourned, but she knows how to fortify."

"Maria's off gathering more wood for the long night ahead," Charlie whispered, motioning to cover their devices, now attached to their forearms for the duration of the survival games. "Heschel and I both agree, tonight we do more than scout the hillside. We do it all. Search. Dig. Retrieve. All or nothing."

"What about Maria? Do you think she knows?" Joanna asked.

"That hadn't crossed my mind," said Charlie. "Why? Do you think she's a spy, too? How could she have known we would say yes to letting her join?" For the first time, uncertainty wrinkled his voice. "That would mean The Chamber doesn't trust me either."

"I don't know about any of that. It just seems odd that not only is this her first Sojourn, but her entire team got sick, and not one of us had heard anything about it," she looked hard at Heschel. "A group of sick students and no newsflash? No quarantine? Hardly anyone gets sick around here."

"Listen, even if she is, we have it covered," Heschel

clarified as Maria returned with an impressive bundle of dry branches.

"That's fantastic, Maria!" said Charlie. "Why don't you join us while the water boils. We're setting our plan for tonight's reconnaissance round."

"What's that?" she said, tossing her bundle on a pile of branches now nearly waist-high—another barrier on the west side of the campsite.

"On the first night, teams are allowed to do a fair amount of recon—info gathering—with little monitor engagement. It's a way of giving each team a chance to catch their bearings without much opposition, yet without total freedom to walk right into another team's campsite."

"It's all about stealth and observation," added Heschel. "We'll want to find out where the key flags of interest are, you know, the main Anti-Libertas flag worth the most notable social points, followed by a handful of minor flags: the fist, the hammer, the sickle, the eye, and the coiled snake."

"Maria, I'm assigning you to be lookout right here at basecamp," said Charlie, sounding more and more like an experienced soldier than a student Interpreter. "Maintain the fire. It's supposed to get cold and rainy, so keep it roaring. And keep an ear out for any other teams who might be gathering intel on our location, supplies, etc."

"Sounds simple enough," said Maria, nodding in

agreement with her role.

"Remember, as long as one team member is at basecamp, it can't be ransacked, not even by the monitors," added Heschel, an attempt to cement Maria's reason for staying put while they're out.

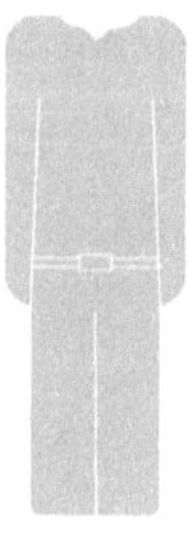

 **16 The Glow**

They leaned toward the fire gripping their mugs tight. Sipping the last remnants of their lemongrass-mint tea, each one put on an extra layer of thermal gear before sliding into clunky waterproof bodysuits.

"They make more noise than I'd like, but if we're going to be worth anything out there, cold and wet, we'll need the layers," said Charlie, bundling up.

Charlie was a notable victor, and teams were always trying to follow in his footsteps—literally. As they were still a good distance from the waterfall, he was fully aware of the need to be cautious, quick, and clear-minded. He knew there would be scouts, both students and monitors, waiting and watching his every move that night.

Maria was settled in by the fire when the others decided it was time to get to work. "You'll do fine," Heschel encouraged her. "Just keep the fire hot and your ears open. We'll be back before you know it." Grabbing their supplies, the small band of rebels headed into the dark. Once at the crest, they headed toward the falls. Dark, with little moonlight and plenty of colorful foliage, there was little chance of running into another student. After all, no one dared to camp this far out on the edge.

They had only been hiking for a few minutes when Heschel paused. "Hold up," he said in a gruff voice from the front of the pack. "Did you hear that? Sounded like branches breaking around us."

"Probably an echo of the branches I'm stepping on," said Charlie. "You seem a little anxious, Hesch. Want me to take the lead?"

The ensuing storm front had pushed the warmth of the afternoon far beyond their reach. Temperatures dropped with the daylight, and winter's cold smell settled in for the first time. An eerie fog rose from the valley below as they worked toward the falls. Like ghostly fingers, it reached up over the edge of the hill separating the three of them from view of one another. Heschel, moving with great but silent strides, extended his lead.

"What is that?" he said, staring through the treeline

ahead. "Is anyone else seeing what I'm seeing? Some sort of glow." Pausing to catch a better look, Heschel discovered his teammates were nowhere to be seen in the fog. It struck him in the dark silence just how lonely it was out there. He had never pinpointed the feeling of loneliness before. After all, students were part of a body of unified bodies. But now, in the cold, dense forest, it became an unsettling reality.

Looks like a flickering fire. He stared at the strange sight. *A camp? No way, I've never seen a fire take that shape before and not out here on the edge. How close is it? It must be near the river.*

The young Observer stood carefully balancing on a narrow boulder jetting over the valley. Watching the glow slowly move within what he could only guess to be a five-foot radius, as though floating in the fog, he was mesmerized.

"You're a hard one to keep track of, you know that?" said Charlie, hopping on the boulder next to him. "What are you looking at?"

"Don't you see it? That glow! Like a floating campfire. Across the river, I think."

Charlie stepped forward, nearly pushing him over the cliff. "I don't see a thing, Hesch. Are you sure it isn't just the moon's reflection or something?

Joanna caught up as the two were staring into the dark. "What did I miss?" she asked, bobbing and weaving, trying to catch a good look. "I see fog and trees and maybe some glistening water. What is it?"

"Wait, it's gone. I've been watching it for the last thirty seconds at least!"

"Is that the river?" Charlie asked with a fresh bounce. "We made it, Hesch. Ahead of schedule. We might just beat the rain after all."

Charlie jogged ahead along the ridge where the trees grew thicker before opening into a clearing about fifteen feet wide on either side of the waterfall.

"Hesch, let's go!" yelled Charlie. "I believe you, but whatever you saw isn't there now. Let's do what we came for. Let's find the rest of that old-world plaque."

Joanna took several slow steps forward, "I want to hear about whatever you saw when we get back to camp, okay? But Charlie's right."

There was no time to waste. They had managed to handle their surprise guest, Maria, without missing a beat. Yet they had no idea how far Principal Chicanery would go to trace them. While they knew that the GPS on their devices was supposed to be off during a Sojourn, they also assumed that Chicanery wouldn't offer them an inch of privacy. The only real mystery was whether or not they would find what they were looking for, and, if so, would they be able to hide it before the monitors caught up with them, or worse, whisked them off to the infirmary.

It was loud near the falls and cold too. The chill had already begun to set in beneath their suits.

"I'll go first," said Charlie, standing beside the falls, eyeing the climb. "Toss me the rope."

Heschel and Joanna froze. "This isn't the plan, Charlie. What happened to the plan?" Heschel was still feeling anxious after witnessing the strange orb moments before. And a little irritated at Charlie's lack of interest.

"Look, I underestimated the dark. These clouds are great for added cover, but they're a nightmare for inexperienced climbers edging and smearing. Overall I've done more top-roping than the two of you combined, and besides, you're acting a little strange tonight." Without waiting, he grabbed the end of the rope and began threading it around his waist, through the carabiners he'd clipped to his leather belt and then in a tight loop with which to grasp. It wasn't a professional tie-in, but he just needed something to lean on for a few minutes at a time.

"Ten minutes," said Heschel.

"I agree. Ten minutes and we rotate," added Joanna. "After all, Hesch knows precisely where he found the stone in the first place."

"Ten minutes," agreed Charlie. "Now weave your end around that beech tree, pull it about 270 degrees and tie it off. It's a crude safety line, but you won't need to belay much since I'll be repelling on my own strength."

"Why didn't we do this last time, Hesch?" chuckled Joanna as she began to flesh out Charlie's plan.

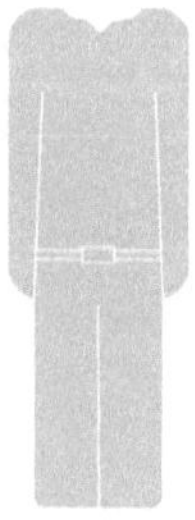

 17 Teamwork

He was cold and wet, squeezing the jagged rocks on the steep, wet dropoff beside the waterfall high above the dark abyss. Now and again, with thoughts of menacing monitors roaming about, Charlie's pace quickened. Ten minutes under this sort of pressure doesn't feel like ten minutes. No, it feels like a day's worth of labor with no end in sight.

Until it slipped from his grip, lost in the chasm below, Charlie's foldable hand trowel did most of the work. Without skipping a beat, he continued pulling and prying on every loose stone he could reach. Swiping away mud and brushing off gravel, he moved like his life depended on it.

"Hesch. Hesch! Secure my rope, tie off another, and join me down here, would you?" barked Charlie over the sound of the crashing water.

"But that's not the plan, Charlie!" yelled Hesch, becoming frustrated with all the changes implemented on the fly. "We switch. I mean, what if one of us gets hurt? Joanna couldn't possibly manage our weight on the lines alone!"

"I need your knowledge down here, and you need more hands for digging. It'll go faster if we're both hard at it. We've got the time, and camp is secure. Joanna's got it covered. She's done this before, right?"

Joanna pointed Heschel toward the slack on the other end of the rope. "He's right. You're needed down there, and the more eyes, the better. We may not have another shot at this."

The red and black woven nylon rope was two-hundred feet long with less than seventy-five in use for Charlie. Heschel made a secondary bend around a nearby tree, tied a loop to sit securely in, and made his way to the crest.

"I think I trust your help in lowering me down more than my ability to repel," said Heschel. "Hold tight and then tie it off once I'm in place. Don't burn more energy than you need to."

Using the tree as a pulley, Joanna lowered him down beside Charlie before tying off the slack on her end. After checking both lines one final time, she made her way into the shadowy shelter of a boulder just above the ridge. With a clear view of her teammates, she sat still, quiet, unsure about the whole ordeal.

"Heschel, I know you're doubting my role in all this right now," said Charlie, confident as ever, "but I'm with you two. There's no turning back."

Heschel squinted, staring into Charlie's eyes. His stomach soured, and his heartbeat rose, but his mind couldn't deny Charlie's reasonable claim. He had proven himself and was clearly invested. After all, they were dangling on the side of a waterfall together in search of a mysteriously forbidden truth about the past. A truth buried deep by the very leaders they were groomed to trust. There was no turning back.

Heschel extended his arm. Charlie did the same. Locking hands, they pulled one another in for a chest bump and a firm smack on the back, followed by a loud grunt. "Let's do this!"

From the shadows above, they heard a sharp laugh. "Seriously? What is it with your kind always smacking and grunting? It's so weird. I don't know, primal or something."

The two laughed as the tension between them broke. Without a moment to lose, they set to work.

"We've got to get closer to the falls," shouted Hesch. "I was nearly leaning into the water when I found it. The spraying water must have done most of the work before getting here. Had we shown up a month later, it would've been lost to the deep."

"Which means if there's another piece to the puzzle, well, we might be a minute or two too late." Charlie furrowed his brow, nodded his head as though responding to the hillside, then scanned the mud closer to the falls in hopes of finding a clue, anything at all that would narrow the search.

The two inched their way to the left, slowly finding their footing with each step. The stones were solid but slick as gravel and water washed beneath each step. Every ten minutes, Joanna's alarm sounded. Calling out from the shadow of her perch, the two would switch sides. She quickly discovered this kept them on their toes, even refreshing them for another stretch.

Their fingernails, soft and splitting from saturation and grit, continued to scrape off the muck one layer after another, dropping unearthed stones into the raging river below.

Once in a while, Joanna would send down a bottle of fresh water or a snack in a small, waterproof case tied to the end of a short paracord she'd thought to bring. Breaks were rushed, but the two eagerly thanked her for her brilliant planning for this part of the mission.

For nearly two hours, they kept at it before Heschel cried out.

18 A Fragment

"Did you see that?" Heschel shouted, pointing above the boulder Joanna was perched beneath. "Did you see the glow? Just like before, only bigger and brighter and right above us all!"

Charlie glanced upward, shaking his head.

"It was there, Charlie. Why would I lie?"

"I don't see anything but my hot breath in this freezing rain, Hesch," Charlie replied, continuing to scrape gravel from the hill. "Seriously, Hesch. Do you see anything floating around? I sure don't. I have no idea what you think you're seeing, but it's not helping."

"I see it, Charlie. I absolutely do," said Heschel, confused by the glow and annoyed by Charlie's condescending response. The fog grew dense as the drizzle thickened. He could hardly see a few feet up the hill, yet the glow shined through. "I can feel it too. A deep, bass-like pulsing. It's like I'm connected to it somehow."

"I think whatever happened to you in the infirmary might have crossed some wires." Charlie sat back with his feet planted on the hill, his legs outstretched as he strained to see this object through the fog. To the right of him, Heschel knelt on a flat stone, wholly engulfed in watching the glow slowly move along the ridge toward the forest in the direction they had come.

"Hesch, I see something," Charlie said, breaking his concentration.

"You see it? I told you! It's like a floating campfire, isn't it? Flickering and flashing."

"Hesch, I can't believe it!" Charlie shouted, grabbing his teammate's shoulder. Pushing off toward the waterfall, he was swallowed up by the fanning spray. He emerged after a few seconds, waving a small, broken stone and shouting hysterically.

Heschel, caught off guard by the commotion, turned away from the glow.

"Look! Look, the symbols are just like the ones we saw." Charlie was loud enough to grab Joanna's attention. "And the broken edge, it's the same, Hesch! We've found another piece of the puzzle. I guarantee these fragmented symbols are going to line up perfectly."

"What's going on down there?" yelled Joanna, stirring from her cold perch beneath the overhang. "Did you finally find something? Are you alright? It's starting to feel a little strange up here like I'm being watched or something!"

"There's more!" shouted Charlie, waving the fragment in the air. "There's a stone face just behind the waterfall. It's covered in mud and seems to be crumbling, but it's definitely an old structure, maybe a pillar? Maybe it's a door frame?"

"Pass it over, Charlie, would ya?" said Heschel, beginning to inch his way closer to the falls.

"I can't believe it. I can't believe there's actually more down here. Joanna, can you believe this? There's a whole history buried in the dirt down here. A history The Chamber's been hiding right beneath our feet." Charlie was now fully engrossed in the hunt and oblivious to his partners.

Heschel, searching the hill above, trying to find Joanna in the thick of it, watched as the glow slowly reappeared out of nothing but fog and rain. At first, it seemed to move further up the ridge as it had before, but then, in what seemed an unbelievable acrobatic maneuver, it swooped out into the air above the valley before vanishing into the night sky with a flash.

"Charlie, the glow! It launched into the air overhead—then poof!" yelled Heschel, his voice crackling with surprise. Just then, the rain kicked up from a drizzle to a nasty pour. It came straight down with a heavy blow. Cold and disorienting. Heschel winced as thick drops pelted him in the face, pricking sharp on his cold cheeks.

Charlie was in his own world focused on the incredible find revealing itself more and more as the rain and spray from the waterfall washed away years of mud and grit. "This fragment isn't big enough to complete our tablet. There's got to be one more piece down here."

"The glow, Charlie! It's real." Cupping his hands around his mouth and shouting in the direction of his friend. "Something isn't right. That glow isn't trying to lead us away, Charlie. I think it's trying to warn us. Something's coming toward us!"

Despite the heavy rain and the fierce fog, Heschel, leaning toward his friend, caught the terrified look in Charlie's eyes as he finally looked in the direction of the disappeared light.

"Heschel!" cried Charlie, leaping toward him. "Look out!"

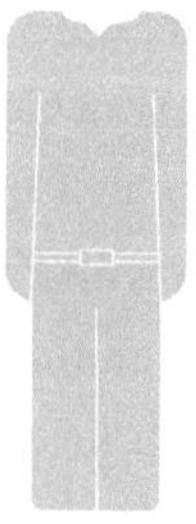

 19 Face to Face

Charlie watched as a mysterious figure swung into view from out of the dark space the light had vanished. It swooped in as though making a grand entrance during the final act of a play. From the corner of his eye, Heschel caught sight of the monitor right before it slammed into his back. It hit with such force that he lost control of both his footing and his grip on the rope. His chest smashed into the muddy hill beside Charlie while his head crashed into a large block of grit-covered sandstone.

"Heschel?" cried Joanna, jumping from her perch to tend to the ropes. "Heschel! What's happening down there? The ropes are shaking and tugging. What's going on?"

"Don't move, Hesch!" Charlie growled, sliding the smooth, black onyx fragment down his friend's collar, deep into his waterproof jumper. "Joanna, I need you to start pulling up Hesch. It's not safe down here. Hurry!"

Having swung in so valiantly, the monitor was viciously trying to regain traction on the wet hillside. Grabbing stones and clumps of loose mud, they threw anything they could at Charlie with a speed and strength quite deceiving based on the small stature of the figure. The monitor was dressed in deputized black and swamp green fatigues with their helmet and face mask dangling behind them, shaken loose from the collision and now awkwardly hanging around their neck.

At the top of the hill, Joanna was frantically trying to get a grip on Heschel's rope. Everything was soaked, and her hands ached from the cold.

What do I do? I'm not trained for this! What am I doing here? Her thoughts inflamed her newfound emotion.

Slipping on mud and turning in circles, that's when it appeared—the strange light. It was exactly as Heschel described, thick with a sort of candle-like glow, yet airy and agile. A floating campfire just out of reach.

What do you want from me? What are you? Joanna broke into a cold sweat, momentarily frozen in place. She was trapped between the terrifying spirit in front of her and the violent confrontation happening on the hillside. "Help me if that's why you're here...please. Or just leave us alone!"

The glow rushed toward her, rose high above her head, then descended directly on top of her shoulders. Immediately her mind was calm and clear. The paralyzing fear had vanished. She knew what she needed to do. It was as though the disorienting sting of the cold had paused. The stormy night had relinquished its oppressive grip. She felt warm, renewed, and fully equipped for this singular task.

Down below, Charlie was losing steam. He had been clinging to that hill for hours, and his muscles were beginning to tremble with exhaustion.

"What do you want with us?" he shouted at the monitor, trying to wrestle another stone from their grip. "Why are you attacking us? I told Chicanery I could handle it."

With a twist of the wrist, the monitor managed to escape Charlie's slick grasp, cracking him across the shoulder with a fist-sized stone. "I'm not here for Chicanery or you or even those other two staying in my old flat. I'm here to finish what I started."

Charlie tried to shield himself from the blow but yelped loudly as the stone hit hard, deeply bruising his upper arm and simultaneously cracking his collar bone. Balancing himself sideways near the falls, he watched in pain as his friend slowly ascended the hill thanks to the blistered hands of Joanna up above. Though still limp and hunched over, Heschel began to groan. One eye opened, searching his surroundings. "Charlie?"

"Hesch! Get out of here before it's lost!" Charlie shouted, chaotically tossing rocks at the monitor. "I don't think I have much more in me. You need to climb. Now!"

"I want whatever it is that you found. Hand it over, and I'll be sure to recommend you for a mild session with the Re-Education Committee. Hand it over now!" yelled the monitor, relentlessly slinging mud and gravel at Charlie's face, waiting for the moment to strike again.

"Hold on a second. Hold on!" he yelled, cheeks scratched and bloody. "I know you, don't I? I know that voice."

The monitor froze. The rain and fog had provided enough cover without their mask, but now, with more talking than they had intended and such close contact, their attempt at discretion had failed.

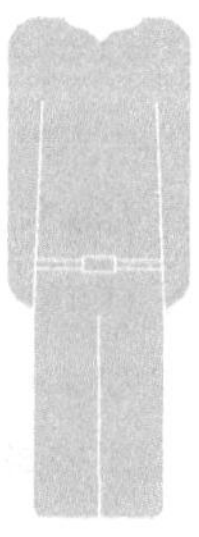

20 Survive

"**M**aria? Is that you?" Charlie's voice crackled with confusion.

"0561?" choked Heschel, coughing up mud and rain. "Monitor...number...0561."

"A monitor? But you're a student," said Charlie, his voice growing hoarse. Losing strength, he fell sideways against the muddy hill, defeated by the reality of her deception. "I've seen you around the compound. How is this possible?"

"You've only seen what they want you to see," she said, letting her guard down. "They started posting my picture on Stream only weeks ago. Pasted into old session photos and included in the daily rotation on governance committee landing pages, session home screens, and throughout the digital updates. You've seen me, and you think you've known me like any other student in any other gray uniform attending any other session. But I'm not. And I'm not the only one."

"Why?" he asked, his voice dropping, more confused than ever before. "If you're not here for Chicanery, then what's your objective? Why do you want what we want?"

Maria grabbed a handful of earth and squeezed as it oozed between her fingers in a mix of mud and blood, the sandstone gravel slicing her skin. Too angry to respond, her teeth ground together with lips unfurled like a dog ready to strike.

Maria, said Heschel, staring at her stern face and trying to connect with her red, watering eyes. His lips didn't move as he attempted to bypass the emotion in his voice and connect with her mind. He could feel the pulse of the glow, though he couldn't see it. He could feel a prompt to connect with her, to try to dig deeper, to find the source of the chaos.

"Who said that?" she called out, her wet hair, shaped exactly like Joanna's, whipping in all directions before turning to meet Heschel's eyes now steadfastly locked onto her own.

Maria, you don't have to do this. I know that you're

looking for answers—the same as us.

She closed her eyes tight, clenching the mud even tighter.

You actually remember your family, don't you? They raised you as a child, didn't they? Longer than most of us before we arrived at Compound 40. And you were sent away. Closing his eyes, he caught a vision of her as a small child wearing the strange sort of long and colorful gown he witnessed in those clips while in the infirmary. He watched her cling to two older people who seemed very distraught, parents maybe, and yet who wouldn't attempt to hold onto her. He could see it so clearly. Deputized monitors picked her up as she thrashed about, carrying her to the van and strapping her down behind tinted windows. An old van filled with whimpering students. He had never seen such emotion before.

"You had a family and traditions—real, ancient traditions," Heschel called out. "And you know about the symbols on the stone, don't you? I saw one hanging on a chain around the neck of the people you were clinging to."

"I don't remember," she cried, tears blending with the rain and mud. "I don't remember, and I don't know what you're trying to do, but I don't trust you. I don't trust any of you. I just want the..."

Seeing a moment of weakness, Charlie leaped from the face of the hill, dove through the air, and tackled Maria, both crashing into a knot of stones like knuckles littered across the hillside. The hit was so intense that his metal belt buckle, strained beyond its load-bearing ability, bent cockeyed, releasing the leather belt around his waist and freeing the carabiners fastened securely only a moment before. The rope holding him had been sliced clean through on impact—pinched on the sharp edge of a sandstone shard. Quick as a thought, it slipped through the carabiners like a snake recoiling from danger. Charlie grabbed hold of the stone jumble and plastered himself against the face of the sopping wet hill. Secured tight by her steady line, Maria sat on his back like an immovable statue.

"Charlie!" Heschel cried out. "Reach up and grab Maria's rope!"

"Charlie, I didn't intend this to happen—for things to go this far," whispered Maria, struggling to support his weight, her hands wedged beneath his armpits. "I just want to find answers to questions I don't even know how to ask. Who to ask."

Charlie clung to the hillside without saying a word, too exhausted to speak. Too disoriented by the pain of his crushed collar bone to respond. Cold, shivering, and losing his grip, he closed his eyes and held tight with his aching, bleeding hands.

"Charlie," Maria whispered, pressing in on his back. "Charlie, just give me the object. We'll all get back safely. I give you my word. You'll complete The Sojourn and maybe even get on with a few extra tokens as a reward. I'll quietly go on serving without a word. We'll all win."

Tears ran down Charlie's cheeks as desires and dreams and the future flashed through his mind. He'd never really thought about what it meant to live a long and worthwhile life. Not with any sort of personal meaning full of passion and purpose. He'd never felt the desire to live. He never had to. Life on Compound 40 simply happened.

Behind him, Maria began drawing deep breaths. An ominous sort of breathing, like a dragon losing its patience.

"I'm going to count to three, and you're going to hand it over," she growled close to his ear, pressing hard on the back of his head, causing mud and grit to wash over his eyes and into his mouth. "If you refuse, I'll drop you into the valley without a care. Then I'll do the same to your exhausted partners one at a time until I get what I came for."

Maria, you don't want to do this, said Heschel, attempting to intervene before her words became a reality. *Your purpose is greater than this. I know it. I can feel it. You don't have to search alone. Look up here. I have what you're looking for. The relic is right here in my suit.*

"One…" whispered Maria, unwilling to trust anything Heschel muttered. The Anti-Libertas mindset was built on obedience. It was one of the leadership's most sought-after values. Trust? It was nothing more than a convoluted emotion, warped and twisted through time and space. Trust fostered weakness. It demanded freedom, give and take, healthy debate, facts, humility. Obedience? Well, it's little more than an *A* or *B* proposition. *A* obey, or *B* disobey. Heschel was not obeying.

Heschel, realizing that his hope for Maria's change of heart was dwindling, quickly diverted his focus. Joanna would have to join in the impossible task of rescuing Charlie.

Joanna, I need you to listen to me.

"Hesch?" she said, nearly dropping the rope. "Where are you? How are you doing that? It's the glow doing this, isn't it? I saw it!"

Charlie isn't going to make it without your help.

"What can I do? If I let go of yours, you'll drop to a sudden stop pretty hard. You can't handle that, can you?"

"Two…" said Maria, squeezing Charlie's arms with a growing rage.

I'll be fine. I've got a good foothold. When I say so, you need to cut Maria's rope.

"I don't know where it's at," she said, voice shaking. "It's too dark. I'll never find it in time."

Look for the glow. I know you can see it. It's the only reason I'm still alive, he said, smiling with a calmness that surpassed his own ability to understand all that was happening. *Let go of my rope and get ready to run toward the glow. I'll be fine. Let it guide you.*

"I didn't think it would come to this, but I warned you, Charlie," growled Maria. Releasing her grip from under his arms, she angrily grabbed hold of Charlie's shoulders. Still clinging to the rocks, he was too tired to resist her maneuvering. She planted her feet on either side of his body just above his waist, and with a guttural yell that echoed through the valley below, she cried, "THREE!"

"Now, Joanna!" yelled Heschel.

The glow had already appeared, now hovering at the base of a tree only a dozen feet away. Joanna, without hesitation, ran and dove toward the tree while pulling her compound-issued pocket knife from its designated position on her waist. In the soft light of the glowing orb, she noticed a glistening rope restrained nearly one foot above the ground and secured at the base of the tree. With the accuracy of a trained soldier under stress, Joanna swiped at the line.

Heschel, I discovered what some of the symbols mean... what the relic says.

"Charlie? You feel the pulse? Hold on! Don't give up. Don't let go, Charlie."

Hesch, it's not like anything I've ever read before.

"You can tell me when we get out of this mess, Charlie. Just hold tight. We've got a plan." Heschel had never felt the weight of the balance between life and death before. Death was always a function. It happened, like a bird coming to the end of its allotted time frame or a leaf falling from its perch in its appointed season. He wasn't prepared for the definitive tone in Charlie's voice, as though he were wrapping up the end of a long story.

It's all broken up, Hesch. Sentence fragments. 'Love me you...what I command...will ask the...and he will... you another...to be with you...the Spirit of Truth...cannot accept.' Hesch, you're going to have to fill in the blanks. Make it count.

Heschel watched Maria pull backward with all her remaining strength just as the tension on the line found relief. Joanna had sliced the rope clean through. Maria's expression turned from rage to absolute terror as she realized her harness was no longer holding her body firmly to the hillside. Thrashing about like a squirrel falling from its perch, she clawed at the air, grabbing hold of Charlie's suit collar. His eyes opened wide, met Heshel's as if to say goodbye, then closed tight as he released his grip, plunging back into the dark abyss without uttering a sound.

Heschel collapsed against the stone face of the hill, took a deep breath, and began to sob.

Up above, Joanna made her way back to Heschel's line and set to work pulling him up. Shaking off the shock, he set his feet firmly on the stone and began to carry his weight. The two met just over the steepest part of the ridge and embraced momentarily before collapsing to the ground.

"Where's Charlie?" she asked.

Heschel shook his head as tears poured out once again. Joanna gasped, leaned back in the mud, and began to cry.

After several minutes Heschel wiped his eyes, pulled the stone fragment from his waterproof suit, and squeezed it with both hands.

"We have to hide this and mark its location in a way that only you and I would subconsciously recognize," he said, calm and professional, like Charlie. Like he'd done this before. "They're going to re-educate us, and they're going to do it with every ounce of tyrannical blood flowing through the system. I don't imagine we'll remember any of this when it's all over, but we need a marker, a trigger, a symbol to remind us in our deepest memories what we've discovered and who we are."

"But what about Charlie? And Maria?" Joanna asked, beginning to cry again. "We can't just leave them."

Heschel turned toward the ridge, wrapped his arms around his knees, and sat in silence beside his friend.

The sun had begun to rise by the time they made it to camp.

"It's been ransacked," said Joanna, too tired to act on her frustration.

Heschel crawled into his tent and stretched out on the hard ground. Shivering, he wiped water from his face and clutched his chest. His heart ached like nothing he'd ever felt. In the red glow of the dawn, he saw a note lightly scribbled across the ceiling of the tent written with mud.

You've done well Heschel - P. CHICANERY

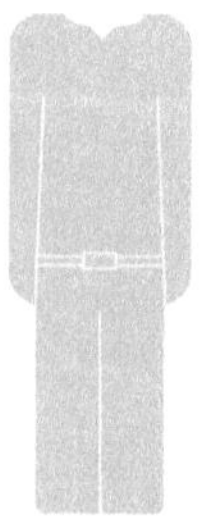

21 It Can't Be

"**W**hat do you think they'll do with us?" Joanna asked. They were passing through the empty courtyard on their way to Chagrin Center. The two students had been ordered to stand in judgment before the Anti-Libertas board.

"Nothing," Heschel replied, watching crows descend on the giant oak tree high above the maples.

"Nothing?" she repeated, watching him watch the birds.

"Do you know what people used to call a flock of crows?" he asked.

Joanna shook her head.

"A murder," he said confidently. "A murder of crows."

"Why do you know this?" she asked, stopping on the

path. "And why are you telling me just before this huge meeting?"

"When a flock of crows descended, people would take it as a mysterious sign of impending doom. Nature's clairvoyant symbol of death and despair." He stepped back to get a better view of the limbs above.

"You're saying we're doomed?" She stepped back in tandem.

"Crows are smart creatures," he continued, staring up at the large black mass swaying back and forth on the uppermost branches. "Sure, they're scavengers, but they mate for life, stay close to family, and defend crows of other flocks when trouble arises."

"So you and I are the crows? Or is The Chamber the murder? I'm lost. Who's scavenging, and who's defending? I don't know how to read this sign, Hesch."

"We're the crows," he smirked, waving her on toward their impending doom.

The sky was blue, and the air was cold, the kind that bites a little when a breeze kicks up. A week earlier, throughout that awful night, it seemed as though the rain and fog and darkness would never end. Though officially disqualified from The Sojourn—with leadership covering up the true events—Heschel and Joanna were more than willing to give it up. For several days they rested side by side in the infirmary, sick with chills, fever, and congestion, yet spared from a session in the re-education room.

"We've become our own murder since all this began, haven't we?" he wondered out loud. "A couple of young crows standing firm in the face of a mighty predator. A scary sight to those in power. In reality, we're just a couple of bumbling students who happened to stumble into an alternative past we know nothing about."

"We're stubborn and maybe immature, but not bumbling," she clarified.

Heschel looked her in the eyes and smiled.

"But I'm not sure I like being called a murderer," she said, as the image of Maria's rope slipping over the ridge flashed through her mind. A memory that's tossed her around in bed each night since.

"What I mean is, crows stick together. We scrape for survival, and we help each other out in desperation." Heschel leaned back, cupped his hands over his mouth, and crowed up into the trees with an unexpected, high-pitched crack in his voice. It echoed off the surrounding buildings causing Joanna to smirk as the birds overwhelmingly replied.

"What if they decide to reassign us, you know, separate us?" she said. "Or how do we outsmart brainwashing? How do we protect one another when our minds are deconstructed? Or worse, end up like Charlie and Maria?"

"Look at that. They're waiting for us," said Heschel,

pointing toward Chagrin Center as confident as Charlie always seemed to be. "If we get to that point, and I don't think we will, but if we do, just listen for the voice below the noise. You've seen the glow. You've experienced its calm. Now you've got to feel it pulse through you as you listen closely for the sound of reason—for its voice."

"The sound of the glow?" She wanted to be more frustrated with him and his mystical reply, and yet, as she imagined the glow that guided her that night, a sort of peaceful understanding came over her once again. Maybe she didn't understand the pulse and the voice, but she knew she could trust him.

"Ahhh, there you are. We've been waiting for the two of you." The bold voice came from a stoic, white-haired stranger dressed in the standard swamp-gray uniform yet highly decorated with dozens of odd-shaped and colored insignia. They were standing by the main entrance watching the students mosey through the yard.

Heschel and Joanna had never seen so many patches and pins on one uniform before and were struck by just how far-reaching the impact of their misadventure must have been. The highest ranks had arrived to intervene firsthand.

The students nodded hello and were passing by when one patch, in particular, caught Joanna's eye. "Excuse me," she said, boldly addressing the elder. Pointing out a stark red and black patch on the breast pocket, she asked, "How did you earn that badge? What does it symbolize?"

"Ahhh, yes, well, when you've traveled to as many compounds as I have, you tend to be in the right place at the right time to earn just about anything worthwhile," they replied, doing little to cover up their annoyance.

"But what does it mean?" she said, her eyes searching the ground as though flipping through an invisible catalog of Anti-Libertas symbols and signs. "It seems so...familiar."

The stranger paused, patience wearing thin. "Young Observer, there are many more compounds, and not all compounds are as structured or as stratified as this one. Unfortunately, social engineering never evolves the same way twice, yet, it always seems to create the same sort of byproduct. And that byproduct requires a special set of skills to manage. I hold those skills. And now I'm here. Do you understand?"

Heschel took a deep breath. *I know you're picturing a relic from the box. I recognized it too, but right now isn't the time to follow that trail, Joanna. I get the sense we'll know more soon enough.* Tapping her on the shoulder and clearing his throat, he prompted her to step back and allow the elder to lead them, without question, into the belly of the Anti-Libertas beast.

"Nevermind," said Joanna, shaking her head. "I'm thinking of something else—something I learned in a session last week."

The elder abruptly turned, entered the building, and

quickly disappeared down the dark hall. With an anxious jump to catch up, the two followed as close behind as they could manage. Thankfully the elder's thick, white hair appeared to glow in the dark, like a floating orb guiding their path. Navigating the maze-like marble halls, Joanna and Heschel stopped keeping tabs on all of the lefts and rights and doors and vestibules—there would be no quick escape should the need arise. The sound of their boots clicked and echoed as the three of them made their way to the center of Chagrin Center.

Four members of The Chamber of Trust were standing behind their respective podiums. Principal Chicanery was positioned dead center on stage in front of the members. The white-haired stranger made their way up the rear steps, coded into their device, then stood at attention behind their podium. Deputized monitors formed a wall behind the leaders. It was an imposing sight, though not necessarily threatening.

The room was round and decorated with marble and wormwood and full of empty hand-carved pews filling the room in twelve concentric circles. Heschel couldn't help but notice how the endcap of each pew was uniquely decorated with strange yet familiar symbols and shapes. Thanks to the stained glass dome on the ceiling, sunlight created a natural glow that shed some of the anxious weight beginning to rest on their shoulders.

"Well now," started Principal Chicanery, "it's a pleasure

to finally introduce our survivors. Elders, meet Wide Awake Heschel and young Observer Joanna."

The remaining members of The Chamber nodded, looking them up and down. They appeared to be unimpressed.

"Principal," urged one council member before an awkward pause. "Considering how they handled your two failed spies, their naivety clearly sets them apart for more, that I have no doubt. However, they aren't much to look at. Nothing more than runts of a Deplorable litter."

"We're not completely naive," blurted Joanna. "I know we're here because of our disobedience. Because we're finding out that the world is bigger and older and stranger than you're willing to let on. Because Charlie and Maria died during our..."

"During our unapproved activities," Heschel calmly cut in. "I know that you spread the rumor about Charlie and Maria being reassigned beyond Compound 40 to maintain order, but what do you want from us? After all, if you were going to re-educate us, you already would have."

Principal Chicanery and the others looked back and forth, nodding.

"Runts?" Chicanery said to the others before clearing his throat in the sort of way that lets the room know who's in charge. Looking back toward the students, he continued, "We want to make you a deal."

"Like you did with Charlie?" Joanna added. "And

Maria?"

"No, not quite like that," he replied, visibly annoyed with her tone. "Not yet. Instead, you'll see a map of the entire property on the screen above. Now, I know you've hidden the relics, and I know they're on site. I know one is indoors, your flat most likely, and the other outdoors between the falls and your campsite..."

"What sort of deal?" demanded Joanna.

"Hand them over, and we'll let you keep up your search for meaning as long as you want."

"On what condition?" joined Heschel. "Why would you let us continue to undermine your history?"

"Don't be a fool, Heschel. You're a bright Wide Awake. That's why you're here. In fact, you're the only student ever to brush off a mild dose of our finest and most prolific re-education therapy," said Chicanery, stepping down from his pulpit and making his way toward them on the floor. "Something interesting happened in that therapy session. Do you recall? Something our equipment recorded for the first time. At first, we thought it was a malfunction, a glitch. But you responded to it, some sort of strange warp in time and space right before our eyes. Of course, we couldn't see what you were responding to. A voice, real or imagined I don't know. We didn't detect so much as a syllable. Yet our equipment registered another presence. You know what I'm talking about, don't you?"

Chicanery locked eyes with Heschel, who remained calm and clear-minded.

"And the earthquake?" said Chicanery, egging Heschel on to confirm his suspicions. "The moment our equipment detected this other presence, the room began to tremble. Strangely, no one else felt it. Not a single person in the rest of the building or throughout our glorious compound felt that tremor. Only the handful of us who were present. And the epicenter? You."

Joanna gasped. She hadn't felt a thing that day. There was so much she didn't know about his time in the infirmary. Anxious, she reached out just to feel Heschel's presence.

"Young lady, there is no touching on this compound!" shouted the white-haired elder that greeted them. Joanna yanked her arm back, trembling. Chicanery whipped around indignantly, glaring at the council member. Each of the other members joined in the glare with palpable intensity. The feeling in the room immediately turned sour.

"I told you I had this taken care of, didn't I?" growled Chicanery as the rest of the members formed a circle heatedly debating the careless gendered slip in pronouns. Unwilling to entertain the roaring debacle onstage between his fellow leaders, Chicanery motioned for the entire council to be escorted out of the great hall with the wave of his hand. The wall of monitors marched into action, calmly but quickly ushering the group out until only Chicanery and the students remained. Without so much as moving a muscle, the three of them stood in silence for several minutes.

"Let's speak bluntly for a moment. What do you say?" Turning his back to them, the powerful leader quietly whispered into the tablet on his forearm. Immediately all three of their devices powered down.

"Lady?" said Joanna. "What did they mean by that? Is that what my kind are called?"

"We won't do it," Heschel cut in, not wanting to give Chicanery the opportunity to manipulate their hearts and minds. To divide them. "We won't accept your offer."

"Heschel, shouldn't we talk about it?" said Joanna, elbowing him in the ribs.

Heschel looked her in the eyes with a compassionate plea for trust once again. *They want what we have. They want to use the glow to find any trace of history and destroy it. No doubt they'll do more than re-educate and reassign us when we're done, when we're useless to them.* Heschel's forehead and cheeks contorted, much like his expression that first night on the hill. Tears rolled down Joanna's red cheeks. *I know I'm asking a lot. I've asked a lot lately. But we marked a clue on the edge for this very reason, didn't we? If we trust the glow, if we listen for that voice, well, I know we'll make it—both of us. And we'll find answers to all of this.*

"Why are you two staring at one another like that?" said

Chicanery, growing impatient at their lack of response and his apparent loss of control. "It's happening again, isn't it? I can see it on your faces. Are you actually communicating with one another? Speak to me. I command it!"

I trust you, she said, wiping tears on her sleeve. *But if I don't hear the voice, if I don't remember anything on the other side...I mean, just don't forget about me, Hesch.*

"Crows, remember?" said Heschel.

"A murder of crows," she whispered back.

"MONITORS!" Principal Chicanery shouted, stamping his feet. His voice bounced around the chamber and out through the halls. "Remove these conspirators, these degenerates, these freedom-hating Deplorables!"

Without delay, the deputized monitors, covered head-to-toe in riot gear, rushed in from all six entryways in the round. The other elders were nowhere to be seen.

"What gives you the right to be so calm in a moment like this?" demanded Chicanery. "Don't you know the power I have over your lives? Don't you know what's coming? I gave you a fair chance, an opportunity for an equitable outcome for all. One and the same - the same as one. And this is what you choose? Selfishness? Disobedience?"

Principal Chicanery paced in circles at the center of the hall tracing the lines of the Anti-Libertas logo imprinted on the floor in speckled red and black granite. His face twisted as he watched the students calmly succumb to the massive entourage ushering them to their doom. Stomping and cursing with a rage he hadn't felt since his youth, Chicanery ripped the device from his arm and hurled it at one of the overhead screens still displaying a map of the entire Compound.

"Where is it! Where is the evidence! Where did you hide it!"

The small, black device smashed into the screen, ricocheted off of a nearby pillar, and bounced down the same hall the students had just departed through. Glass rained from above in a sudden downpour as Chicanery attempted to duck. Losing his balance, he landed face down on the stone logo. Shards of glass covered his back, slicing and scarring his perfectly manicured, tailor-made uniform.

The mass of monitors paused for a brief moment, still holding tight to the rebels now in their trust. They looked back to see their supreme leader in a heap on the floor. They had never witnessed Principal Chicanery lose control. Without a sound and in complete unison, the deputies continued with their task.

When the room was silent, the elder councilman rose to his knees. He was carelessly brushing glass from his shoulders when it caught his attention. A hazy, flickering, orange orb, something like a candle flame, illuminated the dark and barren hallway. For several seconds it hovered just beyond the door frame before disappearing further into the empty passage in the direction of the students.

"It can't be." Principal Chicanery froze. His mind raced through every ounce of history he could recall. *It's back.*

 Epilogue: Translation Unknown

Charlie snuck into the library. The sound of his drab gray uniform scraping the ground was the only noise in the building. The monitors had just finished patrolling the wing and wouldn't be around for another fifteen minutes. As for the rest of the compound? It was just past one a.m., and students, as well as staff, would be asleep for several more hours. No one ever broke curfew. No one had any reason to.

Alright, alright, I need to hold it together, he repeated to himself. *I have plenty of time to make some noise, fire up some computers and tease out this thread of an idea.*

The library functioned more like a museum. The few

that remained, hardback books were kept behind glass—
for viewing, not touching. Besides, no student ever asked
to handle them. All the books they could ever want were
digital and available on their individually assigned tablets.
That said, there were times when researching a topic meant
larger screens, easier access to files across multiple data
chains, and, once in a while, the help of a trained librarian.

Charlie stayed low to ground, below window level just
in case. He knew he was alone, but he had never done
anything like this. *How on the edge did Hesch and Joanna
make their way across the entire compound and back
without getting caught?* Sweat ran down his neck, pooling
up along his collar.

After staring far too long at an old Encyclopedia
Brittanica on display, he put his head down, kept low, and
shuffled to the desk at the center of the room. His heart was
racing. Sweat beaded up along his brow, running into his
eyes, making seeing in the dark more difficult.

Breathing deep, he pulled his knees in close, planted his
feet on the hard floor, and slowly rose to begin his search
on the central system.

"Charlie?" squealed a voice that seemed to echo through
the halls.

"Blaaaagh!" spewed Charlie, falling back with a crash
against a metal case behind him. "Who is it? What are you
doing in here?" he barked.

"I…I'm…I'm a volunteer! I'm always here." the student whimpered from behind the desk.

"It's past curfew," he replied, mustering up his most professional-sounding tone. "Who permitted you to enter the library after hours? To use the main system without oversight?"

"I…well…I like to work in silence. You know, without distraction," said the student, his voice quivering though sounding more confident with each word.

"Stand up. Present yourself." Charlie stood at attention. His gray uniform grew darker around the collar and more noticeable in the faint glow of the computer screen.

The student grabbed the desktop. First, his short dark hair appeared to rise like the moon over the edge and just as slow. Next, his shoulders until his nametag was visible. Charlie, patiently waiting like a seasoned colonel, recognized the student.

"It looks like we have something in common, Ming," said Charlie.

"You know who I am?" Chih-ming's eyes grew wide as his shoulders dropped.

"And you know who I am. That makes us even as far as being up after hours is concerned." Charlie pulled out a chair, sat, and breathed deep and slow. "Come on, let's talk about how we're going to move forward without ruining my reputation and your private workspace."

Chih-ming leaned back, stretched out his arms, and got straight to the point. "What can I help you with, Charlie?"

"If you were looking to translate a language you're not familiar with—a language no one is familiar with these days—where would you begin?" Cracking his knuckles and tipping his chair back, Charlie watched Chih-ming's expression rapidly change from surprise to curiosity to action.

"Well, the first thing I'd do is take a look at the script and…."

"Nope. No images, no text, no ledger. No evidence," said Charlie, dropping forward in his chair.

Chih-ming sighed deeply. His eyes moved back and forth as though searching through a series of files in his mind. "Alright, we'll start from scratch. Choose one symbol that you can recall, maybe something repetitive, then we'll see what I can dredge up behind Stream on the chain."

"So you'll help?"

"It's gonna take some time, but I've found some pretty interesting stuff in the system," Chih-ming said with a smirk. "You'd be surprised at just how many unique transactions have been overlooked on the ledger. Each one loaded with private information. And the Libertas Token isn't the only one in use either. Charlie, there's a hidden database right here on the Stream!"

"I just need something clear and concrete before the fall

Sojourn. What do you think?" said Charlie, smiling back.

"I think The Chamber of Trust ought to be kept out of the loop on this one. Don't you?"

www.ingramcontent.com/pod-product-compliance
Lightning Source LLC
Chambersburg PA
CBHW032012120726
47902CB00014B/2093